"Maggie, use your head," Peter said. "I'm not spying. I want to see you."

"*I* don't want to see *you*. And I *can't* be seen with you. You're the political enemy, even if you aren't spying, which I doubt."

"Okay, we'll go someplace where we can't be seen."

"The deep dark woods?" Maggie said sarcastically, but she felt her resolve fading.

"How about your home?"

"No!" Maggie almost yelped, thinking of her client's campaign papers spread all over the place.

"What about mine?"

"That's even worse," Maggie said. "What will you do if I don't meet you?"

"The flowers and balloons were only the beginning. There are those streamers they tow behind biplanes, and—"

"Okay, I'll be at your apartment tonight at eight."

Dear Reader:

Happy holidays! All the best wishes to you for a joyful, loving holiday season with your family and friends.

And while celebrating, I hope that you think of Silhouette Romance. Our authors join me in wishing you a wonderful holiday season, and we have some treats in store for you during November and December—as well as during the exciting new year.

Experience the magic that makes the world so special for two people falling in love. Meet heroines who will make you cheer for their happiness and heroes (be they the boy next door or a handsome, mysterious stranger) who will win your heart. Silhouette Romances reflect the magic of love—sweeping you away with books that will make you laugh and cry, heartwarming, poignant stories that will move you time and time again.

During the next months, we're publishing romances by many of your all-time favorites such as Diana Palmer, Brittany Young, Lucy Gordon and Victoria Glenn. Your response to these authors and others in Silhouette Romances has served as a touchstone for us, and we're pleased to bring you more books with Silhouette's distinctive medley of charm, wit and—above all—*romance*.

I hope you enjoy this book and the many stories to come. Come home to Silhouette romance—for always!

Sincerely,

Tara Hughes
Senior Editor
Silhouette Books

OCTAVIA STREET

November Returns

Silhouette *Romance*

Published by Silhouette Books New York

America's Publisher of Contemporary Romance

To my namesake, Octavia McAllister,
without whose hard work, wit, charm,
talent, beauty and modesty this book
and a lot of other things would not
have been possible.

Thanks to Chris Adessa,
campaign consultant and Speakerette extraordinaire;
to Ross Travis of the San Francisco
Registrar of Voters Office;
and to Pacific Bell.

SILHOUETTE BOOKS
300 E. 42nd St., New York, N.Y. 10017

ISBN: 0-373-08612-1

First Silhouette Books printing November 1988

All the characters in this book are fictitious. Any
resemblance to actual persons, living or dead, is
purely coincidental.

®: Trademark used under license and
registered in the United States Patent and
Trademark Office and in other countries.

Printed in the U.S.A.

OCTAVIA STREET

has lived and traveled in Europe, Asia and the Middle East, but she always comes home to her favorite city, San Francisco. She lives in a restored Victorian gingerbread house, which survived the Great Earthquake of 1906, but which might now collapse from the weight of the books inside. She is unable to pass a bookstore or library, even if the books are in a language she doesn't know, which is almost all of them. Her favorite mode of transportation is walking, especially along the magnificent coast of northern California.

Quotation in the marriage ceremony are from
The Book of Common Prayer
According to the Use of the
Espiscopal Church.

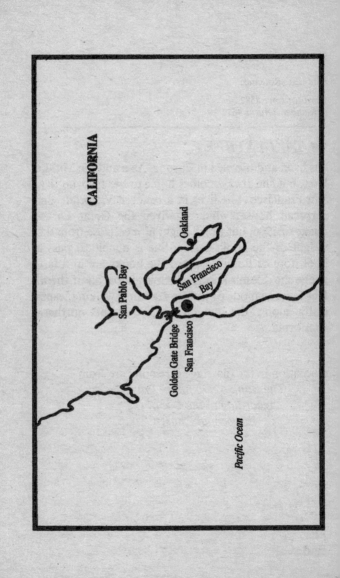

Chapter One

A head appeared around the door with the words McGraw and Associates in gold on the glass and said: "Hey, Mag, hold this open while I wheel in the new filing cabinet."

"I'm going to have to put you on hold for a moment," Maggie McGraw said to the prospective client on the other end of the telephone. "I, uh, have an important call coming in." She pushed a button, stood up, ran a hand through her already tousled red hair and, kicking off her shoes, pulled back the door as far as it would go. The filing cabinet entered magisterially on a red dolly, pushed by a young man with a great deal of hair and small round gold-rimmed glasses.

The filing cabinet had four drawers, as ordered, and was made of an ugly yellowish wood. "Where did you find *this*?" Maggie asked. "It's horrible."

"Secondhand store. You said to try there first. It was only twenty bucks, Maggie." The young man's voice came close to cracking.

"I suppose we could paint it," said Maggie. "Or wallpaper it. Well, anyway, put it over there by the other one. I've got somebody on the phone. Possible client."

But when Maggie got to the phone there was no flashing hold light, and when she picked it up all she heard was a dial tone.

"Oh, damn it, Ted. It's all your fault."

Ted, the young man with the hair and glasses, who was the "Associates" listed on the door, said, "Huh?"

"We just lost another client, and if you hadn't asked me to hold the door it wouldn't have happened. I tried to put him on hold, and hung up on him instead."

"Maggie, I had the filing cabinet you wanted and I couldn't get it in the office. How was I supposed to hold the door, too?"

"You are supposed to have four hands, Ted. What am I paying you for?"

"To take all the blame, and you aren't paying me enough. I quit."

"Fine," Maggie said cheerfully. "Now let's fill up the filing cabinet, and then I'll buy you a drink—if you'll loan me the money."

The offices of McGraw and Associates, political campaign consultants, were singular, just like the associates themselves. They consisted of one smallish square room, with a receptionist's desk by the door and a larger desk and chair at the back, behind a flimsy room divider that was meant to simulate privacy for clients, if any. On each wall were long tables, and all of them were piled high with papers. The walls themselves had once been painted white, but the original color was no longer visible. Posters, calendars and odd pieces of paper were pinned to them as high as the average human could reach. A personal computer stood next to the window, with a printer beside it. The view from the uncurtained window was of the sixth floor of a glossy high rise, a hundred feet away across California Street. Ted and Maggie could look directly into the windows of one of the largest law firms in San Francisco. They had come to know all the employees there by sight. The office of McGraw and Associates was on the top floor of one of the few old buildings left in the financial district. Six floors directly below McGraw and Associates, at street level, was Hennessey's Bar and Grill.

Ted pulled out the bottom drawer of the filing cabinet and groaned. "No wonder it was so heavy. This drawer's full."

"Full of what?" Maggie asked, coming closer to inspect it.

Ted pulled out a folder and opened it. "It's somebody's personal papers!"

"Peter Thomas Barnes," read Maggie. "Those are diplomas, certificates. Look, he went to Yale."

"I wonder how old he was when he died," Ted said.

"What makes you think he's dead?" Maggie asked, sitting down on the floor and pulling out a folder.

"I don't think he'd have sold these with the filing cabinet otherwise. Do you?"

"I suppose not. He wasn't very old, though, only thirty-six. Here's his birth certificate. Born in Rhode Island. Gee, what a waste of a young life."

"These are all letters. Legal stuff. Probate court. He must have inherited some money."

"Look. Love letters," Maggie said. She sniffed. "Perfumed, too."

"You should be ashamed of yourself, Maggie. Reading personal stuff like that."

"I am *not* reading them. I am looking for Peter Thomas Barnes's address, so we can return these."

"Or his heirs' address."

"Holy smoke," Maggie burst out. "Look at this. Do you suppose this is—was—Mr. Barnes?" She held up a photograph of a well-built, darkly tanned blond man on the deck of a sailboat. She could not see his eyes—they were shaded by dark glasses—but the rest of his features were in as fine a configuration as she'd ever seen. Strong but aristocratic. She turned the picture over. P.T.B., *Westwind II*, Newport was written on it.

"Handsome devil," said Ted.

"Is there a marriage certificate in there?" Maggie asked innocently.

"You have no respect," Ted chided her. "But, no, there isn't. Why do you want to know, anyway?"

"Because his wife would be his closest relative," Maggie told him haughtily.

Maggie's knees were beginning to ache. "Put it all back and let's go. It's five o'clock, anyway. We'll figure out what to do with it in the morning."

Maggie helped Ted put the late Mr. Barnes's files away and then spent a few moments trying to get herself in order. As always, the tail of her paisley blouse had come out of her gray wool skirt, and she had been sitting on her suit jacket all afternoon, so it looked like a well-used shopping bag. There was nothing to be done about her fiery red hair, which did as it pleased. At least she didn't have to do anything at all about her green eyes, with their amazingly long lashes. She could always hope that people would notice them, and not the sprinkling of freckles over the small but definite nose and high cheekbones.

Peering into the compact mirror she kept in her desk drawer, Maggie remembered her solemn vow: the next person who took in all her features and said, "Are you Irish?" was going to get a bottle broken over his head. Or so Maggie always said, but she'd never had a bottle handy at the appropriate moment.

"Okay," she said to Ted, who had been lounging by the door. "Let's go."

She locked the door, and together they took the ancient creaking elevator down to the lobby, where they nodded to the security guard behind his scratched desk on the moth-eaten carpet and rounded the corner into Hennessey's Bar and Grill.

The grill had disappeared years before, but the bar remained. Hennessey's was very popular with the after-work crowd in the financial district. It was dark and somewhat dingy, but you couldn't see the latter because of the former. What everyone liked about it was what it didn't have: it didn't have music and it didn't have ferns. The bartender was reasonably pleasant and the cocktail waitress reasonably good, as long as you didn't ask for a drink with nine ingredients, and no one ever did. Hennessey's had been in the same place since 1907, the year after the great San Francisco earthquake. Nobody knew where it had been before that, but it had been somewhere, everyone was sure.

Maggie and Ted found seats at a table immediately, though the place was rapidly filling up, and after orders had been taken, Ted said, "Those papers bother me a lot. We'd better get them back to whoever they belong to."

"How do you suggest we do it?" Maggie said, ducking as a tall customer went by behind her.

"Well, while you were fixing your face—"

"I *never* fix my face."

"While you *weren't* fixing your face, I looked Peter Thomas Barnes up in the phone book. Nobody listed by that name at all. In fact, there are only two columns of Barneses. We could call them all, maybe."

"Maybe. Or you could go back to the secondhand store and find out where that filing cabinet came from."

"What if it's an estate sale?"

"What's an estate sale?" Maggie asked, taking her drink off the waitress' tray. To the waitress she said, "Ted's paying," and nodded in his direction.

"I am?" Ted had a startled expression on his round face.

"I invited you for a drink if you paid. Remember? I haven't got any money."

"I've only got four dollars," he said, fumbling with his billfold.

"Perfect. That'll pay for the drinks, and I'll loan you busfare home," said Maggie. "Just as soon as we get a big job, like a senatorial campaign, I'll pay you back and give you a big raise."

Ted handed over the contents of his wallet and sighed. "And when is that, pray tell?"

"Any day now, any day. Election day is only six months off."

"I don't know why I stick around."

"Because you love the work," Maggie told him. "Now, what's an estate sale?"

"They just auction off everything in the decedent's estate. It usually means there aren't any heirs, or that none of them care."

"Poor Peter Thomas Barnes. What if it was an estate sale? What do we do with the stuff then?"

But Ted was looking over Maggie's shoulder as if he had seen a ghost. Maggie twisted around in her chair until she could see the doorway. Standing there was a tall blond man with chiseled features and an annoyed expression. Put sunglasses on him and you had the man on the deck of the *Westwind II* in Newport. It could only be Peter Thomas Barnes, Maggie decided. Very much alive.

"I think our problem is solved," she said, waving wildly. "Over here."

The tall man threaded his way through the crowd, and when he reached the table he smiled politely. "Are you Maggie McGraw?"

Maggie nodded, dumbstruck. He was even better-looking up close. Even Ted was blinking a bit behind his glasses. Maggie rearranged her blouse at the neck.

"I think you have my filing cabinet, and the contents thereof. Or so the secondhand store told me."

"I do, I do," said Maggie. "I take it you want it back."

"Only the contents," he said. "Oh, forgive me. My name is Peter Barnes."

"I know," said Maggie. Then: "I'm so glad you're alive, Mr. Barnes."

"Pardon?" he said, clearly puzzled. "Alive?"

There was a long, awkward silence while Maggie tried to think of a way out of the corner she had just painted herself into. Then she brightened and, waving her hand across the table, said, "This is my associate, Theodore Post. He'll explain."

But her associate was polishing his glasses with a cocktail napkin and seemed to be whistling. And he definitely hadn't heard what Maggie had said. Definitely.

"Uh, in that case, Mr. Barnes, why don't you just, uh, find a chair and join us in a drink?"

"I don't think so, Miss McGraw. But thank you anyway. I have to be getting on. Just let me give you my card, and you can messenger the stuff to my office tomorrow. I trust it's intact?"

"You would have to decide that," Maggie said. "But how did it come to be in a filing cabinet that got sold? I presume that's what happened."

"Mix-up between my secretary and myself. It was my fault. I was supposed to get my personal stuff out of there, and I forgot. We got new office furniture," he explained with a smile that revealed straight white teeth, and a dimple.

Maggie's neck was getting stiff just from looking up at him. But he, in turn, seemed to be doing a lot of looking down at her—or at least she hoped he was.

"How did you find it so fast, Mr. Barnes? We only got it an hour ago."

"The filing cabinet left my office this morning. I realized my papers were missing at midafternoon, called the secondhand store, found the cabinet had been sold to you and came over here. Your office was closed, but the security guard told me where you were."

"Nice piece of detective work. We—Ted, really— just tried looking you up in the phone book."

"I'm not there yet. I'm new in town. You'd never have found me, but thanks for trying."

"You're welcome," said Maggie. "You're sure you won't have a drink?"

"No, thanks," he said with that dazzling smile. "I really must go. Oh, yes, here's my card. Just use your regular messenger service."

"My regular messenger service," muttered Maggie, who never used any messenger service other than Ted. She looked at the card. It read:

Peter T. Barnes
Corporation Law

3600 Embarcadero One
San Francisco, CA 94111   Sutter, Fenner, Mills
(415) 555-9919   Markward and Peabody

Embarcadero One was as fancy a business address as one could have, and Sutter, Fenner was such a well-known law firm that even Maggie had heard of it.

Maggie quickly dug in her purse. "My card," she said, handing him the very last one she had. "I'll send your files first thing tomorrow."

He put the card in his pocket without looking at it and turned to go. Then he swung around again. "Do you mind if I ask you a personal question?"

"Not at all," said Maggie, blushing prettily, she hoped.

"Are you Irish, by any chance?"

The next morning, for some reason she couldn't quite fathom, Maggie took great care with her clothes—a green silk dress that several men had said matched her eyes—and her hair, which she put into a kind of flyaway French twist that several women had said reminded them of Katharine Hepburn. Then she ate a hearty breakfast, sitting at her little table in her apartment kitchen, with its splendid view of the western end of the city and of the Pacific Ocean. Maggie always knew when the weather was going to be foggy, because she could see it coming on the horizon.

Maggie's view was not at all fashionable. The really expensive views were of the Golden Gate Bridge and the Marin Headlands and Alcatraz, for instance. But Maggie felt her view was at least as good. And the only reason she could afford any view at all was that she had been living in this same rent-controlled apartment for—what was it?—seven or eight years. If her rent had gone up with inflation, Maggie would have been evicted long ago.

She finished the morning paper, got another cup of coffee and waited for her brain to kick in. Then she began her morning ritual: planning the day. She did not like to do this at the office.

This time, however, she was planning her year, which, in effect, was planning the rest of her life. She remembered the bottom line of the calculations she had made a year ago. Unless she got a really good job this year—not these little local things—she would have to declare bankruptcy and, of course, give up her wonderful apartment. And move into some place with no view at all, and get what Ted referred to as "a real job." Typing or selling perfume or something, she thought, shuddering. So much for her dreams of being a big-time political consultant.

But this was the big year, the presidential-and-every-other-office election year. She already had two small clients, one of them a candidate for the city's board of supervisors, another for the county office in San Mateo. But she needed a really big one, a congressman or even—hope against hope—a senator. Perhaps she should go looking for possible candidates. Perhaps she should send a mass mailing to everyone over thirty-five in the Bay Area. "Want to run for the Senate? Let us help."

She sighed, shook her head and took another sip of coffee. What she really needed to do was learn how not to hang up on people. That would be the first order of the day, because she needed to make some phone calls. Then she must not forget to send back Peter Barnes's files. That was easy enough. What wasn't easy was forgetting about him. She admitted to herself that she'd been thinking about him ever since she'd seen the contents of that file drawer. She had, she remembered, even dreamed about that fabulous face, that dazzling smile. And she could not imagine anything less productive than thinking about Peter Barnes. She would never see him again. She would ship his files off via messenger, and never again would she have any reason to even think about him.

And, she scolded herself, she ought to know better. Especially about good-looking men, even good-looking men who might possibly have sailboats. She had practically had it tattooed on her forehead two years ago: Remember Jim. She had vowed to fall in love with a short, appealingly ugly, poor man. But, she had discovered, they were in short supply.

Without thinking, she poured a third cup of coffee, and as she did her wristwatch caught her eye. It was nearly nine. And she would be late. She was the boss, and she believed that the boss should always be there first, to set a good example. Even if the only employee was Ted, who did not respond to good examples, or much of anything else.

Taking a critical glance at the western horizon and deciding that it wasn't going to rain, she grabbed a sweater and her attaché case and tore out the door. A brisk half-block walk brought her to the bus stop, and within seconds a 38 Geary Express had stopped to scoop her up. She stood swaying in front of an elderly man reading a Chinese newspaper and a teenager with a Walkman who was singing aloud to music known only to his ears. Maggie read none of the book that she always carried in her purse to read on the Muni, as everyone called the Municipal Railway, San Francisco's public transit system. She got a seat two blocks before her stop. She considered this a good omen. That meant something nice would happen today.

Ted, wearing the most hideous Hawaiian shirt Maggie had ever seen, was already there, putting Peter Barnes's files into two shopping bags for delivery.

"Haven't we got anything better than shopping bags? That's tacky," Maggie said, recoiling.

"Nope," said Ted.

"Haven't you got some other shirt you can wear to work?" Maggie asked.

"Nope," said Ted.

Maggie made her phone calls. Everyone was in a meeting.

Waiting for the messenger service, Maggie keyed the data into the computer on Carol Gold, the San Francisco supervisorial candidate. She ran a program, SPSS Chi square, and found, among other things, that eighty percent of the San Francisco electorate had never heard of Carol Gold and that that figure was accurate within five percentage points either way. It had come out the same way by hand yesterday. Obviously, Carol Gold had a problem. But all problems were solvable in this business if you had enough money. Carol Gold could become the best-known face in San Francisco. Maggie sighed loudly. But on the amount of money Carol Gold had, that wasn't going to happen. No billboards, no TV spots for Carol Gold.

Maggie fooled around with the PC a little longer, trying to wring every bit of information out of it that she could, and then began writing a suggested campaign—three of them, in fact, each depending on the level of funding.

The man from the messenger service appeared, and he was not at all taken aback by the shopping bags. Ted handed them to him as if they used such services twice a day.

The phone rang, and both Ted and Maggie leaped for it. It was a wrong number.

Then it rang again, and Maggie let Ted answer.

"McGraw and Associates. Yes. Just a minute, please."

Ted put his hand over the receiver. "Are you available? It's Fred Oliver."

"Who is Fred Oliver?"

"He says he's campaign chairman for Charles Portnoy."

"Of course I'm available!"

Maggie leaped for the telephone, and while Ted shuffled his feet and punched buttons at random on the computer—which beeped at him by way of objection—Maggie took notes and tried to keep pace with the rapid-fire voice at the other end of the phone.

After hanging up, Maggie sat back in her chair with a stunned look.

"Well?" asked Ted.

"Charles Portnoy is running for Congress, in the Fifth District. His campaign chairman wants an analysis of a survey they did, and if it's good enough they'll want to hire us for the whole campaign. They are sending the survey over by messenger now, and it is to be done by Friday. Ted, if we get this, we're in business."

"Who is Portnoy running against?"

"Nobody, yet. The incumbent is retiring, and nobody else has declared."

"Just let me get my hands on that survey," Ted said. "That's what you hired me for." Maggie could see that, behind all the hair and glasses, Ted's face had lighted up. Ted could massage facts out of survey results that no one else ever suspected were there. He was a statistics major who had offered to work for practically nothing just for the chance to play with the figures. He had said he would work four months, but here it was nearly two years later and Ted was still an—or rather *the* associate in McGraw and Associates. Looking over at his eager face, Maggie felt a warm spot in her heart for Ted. She smiled benignly at him.

He reached in his pocket and pulled out a piece of paper. He handed it to Maggie. "Since you have a big job, here's what you owe me," he said.

Maggie was horrified to see that it totalled over a hundred dollars. "Drinks, carfare, newspaper, carfare, personal loan..."

"You can pay me in installments," Ted said.

"Monthly?"

"Daily."

"I'll go to the bank on my lunch hour."

At that point the phone rang again.

Maggie grabbed it. "McGraw and Associates, Maggie McGraw speaking." It was the San Mateo County candidate, Harley Davis, a man who needed to have his hand held at all times. Maggie was just saying, "...but there's nothing to worry about. There's nothing to *do*. The election is a full six months away...." when the other line rang. Ted began waving frantically at Maggie.

"Harley, I've got another important call. I'll just put you on hold. Be back in a minute," Maggie said, pushing the wrong button. Harley Davis was cut off.

On the other line, Maggie heard: "Peter Barnes here."

Maggie had discovered that at the sound of his voice her heart had leaped up into her throat and stuck there, making speech all but impossible. At least she managed a syllable that sounded like "Glrrp."

"Do you remember me? I'm the person whose papers you delivered this morning."

"Ahemmmm. Yes, of course, I remember."

"I was wondering if we might be able to get together sometime."

"Ahemmmm. Certainly."

"Do you have a cold? You don't sound well."

"Ahem. No, no, just a frog in my throat. Frog, gad, what a silly expression. I wonder why we say that? I mean, I have a...a lump, no, not a lump, a *thing* in my throat, that's—" Maggie realized she sounded like a card-carrying idiot. It might have something to do with the fact that she was talking to the handsomest man she'd ever seen, and that he seemed to be asking her out.

"Are you free for lunch?"

"Lunch when?" said Maggie, looking at her blank calendar. She would have preferred dinner, but lunch would do.

"Would it be presumptuous for me to ask if you could make it today? I'm in something of a hurry."

Maggie thought it either presumptuous or exciting or both. She said, as coolly as possible, "Yes, I guess I can squeeze you in today. How about one?" Maggie had read that one o'clock was the power lunch hour. But she wasn't sure where the power lunch *place* was, so she said, "Where?"

"Do you know Rick's?"

Maggie didn't know Rick's, except it was in the Embarcadero Center and very, very yuppie. Or, as the new word would have it, very, very DINKy. Double Income No Kids couples went there. Maggie herself, of course, was One Income No Kids. OINK.

Maggie did what any decent OINK would do. She lied.

"Of course. I've been there many times."

"Meet you there at one, then."

"Then till then, then." Maggie hung up before she could say anything even sillier. She needed time to get her heart back in its normal place, working at its normal rhythm. At least now she knew why she had been compelled to dress her best. And she knew what the good omen had been about.

"You look funny. You're all red," Ted said in a friendly manner. "Also, you hung up on Harley Davis. One of your two fer-shure clients."

"Ted?"

"What?"

"Shut up," Maggie explained.

Chapter Two

Rick's Café Américain, which purported to be a copy of the bar of the same name in the movie *Casablanca*, came close enough that you half expected to see Humphrey Bogart seated at a table with Ingrid Bergman. The man at the piano played "As Time Goes By" every third song. It was very, very crowded, but Maggie told the headwaiter that she was meeting Mr. Barnes and found herself whisked immediately across the room to where he was sitting at a window table. He stood up as she approached, and she saw for the first time that his eyes were a tawny brown, under very dark brows, a total mismatch with the sun-streaked blond hair. It was smashing, so smashing that Maggie stopped dead in her tracks. Was there no end to the gorgeousness of this man?

"Is something wrong, modom?" the headwaiter asked, jarring Maggie back to reality.

"No, no, just stopped to, uh, get my second wind," Maggie told him. The headwaiter gave her a now-I've-heard-everything look and pulled her chair out for her. She sat down gratefully.

"Good of you to come," said Peter Barnes, straightening his conservative regimental-stripe tie.

"My pleasure," Maggie replied, pulling down the cuffs of her sleeves.

"And how are you?" Peter Barnes unbuttoned the top button of his Brooks Brothers-or-better suit coat.

"Oh, I'm fine, thank you. And you?" Maggie crossed her legs, right over left.

"Fine, thanks." Peter Barnes unbuttoned the second of three coat buttons.

Maggie crossed her legs left over right and vowed not to let another cliché escape her lips. So she said, "Nice weather we're having."

Peter Barnes took a deep breath, let it out slowly and said, "Care for a drink before lunch?"

Maggie shook her head, though she knew that a good OINK would have ordered a glass of wine, probably white.

"Good day for clichés, isn't it?" said Peter Barnes, and Maggie nodded vigorously, afraid to open her mouth for fear another might fall out.

The waiter came to their rescue. Maggie ordered Dover sole, and Peter ordered oysters and grilled salmon. After all the hustle and bustle of serving was over, Peter Barnes leaned over the table and said, "You must be wondering why I asked you here today, Miss McGraw."

Maggie's heart began to flutter a hundred to the minute. "Please, call me Maggie," she answered, trying not to blush.

"And you must call me Peter," he said as Maggie gazed helplessly into those tawny eyes. But he seemed to be looking over her shoulder as he continued, "I've agreed to act as finance chairman for a friend of mine who is running for office next November. I saw your card last night, and it occurred to me that it might be wise to take your firm into consideration. We're looking for a campaign consultant. I told him that I'd see what you had to say."

During this speech, Maggie's heart fell to her shoes, and then lay there shattered for about twenty seconds. Then it registered on her that even if he wasn't throwing himself at her feet, Peter Barnes might be the key to her success. She could end up with Charles Portnoy and with another big campaign, all in the same week. So what if the world's handsomest man had asked her out for business reasons. It could be very good for business!

"If you have any figures, I can give you some estimates and suggestions in a day or two," she said hastily.

"No, nothing that formal, at least yet.... I just want to know a bit about you and your organization. You'll have to remember that I'm new at this myself. Which brings me to this question: aren't you rather young to be doing this? How much experience do you have?"

Maggie sighed. "I'm older than I look. I'm twenty-nine, going on ninety. I've been in this business eight years, which shows you I don't have all my marbles. I majored in art history in college. Then I worked for a genius named Clint Kelley for six years, until he died. Two years ago I struck out on my own." She concentrated on her salad to give him time to digest that. Her chosen field was one full of hard-drinking, cynical old pols and fanatical young computer jocks. There were not all that many young women to be found in it. She would always stick out like a sore thumb. And that was not necessarily an advantage.

But when she looked up, Peter Barnes seemed both sympathetic and interested. "I heard about Clint Kelley. He's a legend. They copied his methods everywhere. To be honest, we knew you had worked for him, and that was a tremendous recommendation."

"I hope I can live up to it," Maggie said fervently. And then it dawned on her that he had obviously been checking on her. And she didn't know anything about him. Except that he was from the East, a Yale graduate, and that he sailed and worked in corporation law.

"Now that you know all about me—" Maggie began.

Peter interrupted her, saying, "I hope that isn't all there is to know."

She ignored that. This was a power lunch. "I'd like to know more about you."

"Like what?"

"Whatever you want to tell me," Maggie said, feeling impertinent.

"A trial lawyer would say that question needed a foundation. But I'll try. I'm from the east, I moved out here a few months ago, I practice law, I'm single, I don't smoke, I drink very moderately, I don't do drugs, I live in Pacific Heights and I have a cat named Genghis."

"I sort of guessed most of that, except the cat," Maggie said. "I mean other things, like—"

"Like I weighed eight pounds fourteen ounces at birth, my sign is Aquarius and my least favorite city is Philadelphia?" He looked across the table with an inquiring look. "How am I doing?"

"Oh," said Maggie, red-faced and wishing she had never turned the conversation in this direction. It reminded her of a fern bar. "That's nice, but I really wanted to know other kinds of things, like what corporation law is, and what you know about California politics."

"Corporation law is very boring. It's dealing with people who want to incorporate and then helping them afterward. The big, interesting stuff is mergers and acquisitions. As for California politics, I don't know much. I don't think my friend does, either. That's why we need a campaign consultant."

"Why would you do something very boring?" Maggie asked, astonished.

"It's not boring to me." He grinned. "Just to everybody else. But I'm not the issue here. You are." At this he looked directly and, Maggie felt sure, meaningfully into her eyes. "What services can you provide?" he asked.

"Anything you want," Maggie said, leaning forward across the table for emphasis. Her pearl necklace landed neatly in the sauce, clinking on the bottom of her plate. Grabbing her napkin, she quickly wiped it, talking as fast as she could to distract him. It didn't work. She could see him suppressing a grin. "Mornay sauce is wonderful for pearls. I always do that," she tried bravely.

"I'm sure you do," he said solemnly.

"Well, anyway, as I was saying, I'm sort of a one-man show." Maggie slipped her shoes off under the table, for she always thought and talked better barefoot. "Well, except for Ted. And what I can't do, I can hire. A media consultant, a media-time buyer, a pollster, fund-raisers, phone-bank specialist, a direct-mail expert, a data-base company, an opposition-research team. Of course you'd have your own campaign manager. The sky is the limit. Well, actually, the limit depends on you, the finance chairman."

"Good Lord, do we need all that?" Peter looked taken aback.

"If your friend is running for a senate seat in a state as big as California, he'll need more than that—and about six million dollars. If he's running for a less important office, say district attorney, I could do it alone, for a hundred thousand or so. I'm just giving you the parameters, now. It depends on so many things: the office, the candidate, the opposition, acts of God, that kind of thing."

Maggie thought Peter Barnes looked a bit stunned. He had a habit, she noticed, of raising one eyebrow when he did not like what he was hearing. Well, he would have to learn. Anybody else would tell him the same thing.

Suddenly realizing that her feet were bare, she began feeling around under the table with her left foot, trying to locate her shoes.

"Do you have a track record?" he asked. "How well have you done?"

"I've only been in business in one general election, you know. But I have a three-and-one record. And the one loss was a close one." Maggie watched closely. His eyebrow stayed in place.

Just then the waiter sailed up to inquire as to their preferences in regard to dessert. Maggie was relieved. Her track record, though excellent, *was* with small-time offices.

They decided on coffee only, and when two steaming cups had been brought, Maggie asked, "Why don't you tell me a little about your friend?"

"Well, he's never run for office before—"

"That can be an advantage, or a disadvantage," Maggie said, interrupting him. "If he doesn't have a record, nobody can attack him on it."

"That's true," Peter agreed. "It seems to me that his two big advantages are his name, which is an old San Francisco name, and the fact that he can raise plenty of money."

Maggie took a big sip of coffee, tried once again to find her shoes and asked, "What's his name? That's important."

"Sutter. William Sutter," said Peter Barnes.

Maggie thought she might dissolve into little pieces. "Sutter? S-U-T-T-E-R?"

"You've heard of him?"

"No, I've never heard of him, but I know that name." Maggie thought frantically. Sutter was probably the most famous name in San Francisco. There was the Sutter Tower, the Sutter Baths and Sutter

Park, and the name Sutter was to be found on brass plaques and glass doors all over the financial district.

"All he needs to do is get his name on the ballot," Maggie said. "And keep his nose clean. The name is so famous that people will vote for him no matter what. Providing he's not a bigamist, except I doubt that that would hurt him here. Maybe if he had a lot of parking tickets..."

Peter Barnes laughed, showing a row of perfect white teeth. "I'm pretty sure he's not a bigamist, but I don't know about the parking tickets."

Maggie found one shoe under the table and slipped it on. She began scrabbling for the other.

The check arrived, and Peter dropped a credit card on the tray. Maggie thought about her possible fantastic luck that day. If Ted did a terrific analysis of the survey that had been done for Portnoy, she'd have one candidate for Congress. And if she got this one, this William Sutter, she had a sure winner. You couldn't lose with a name like Sutter. Maggie felt sorry for whoever was running against him. She felt around under the table for her other shoe and failed to find it. Then she remembered that she had forgotten to ask a key question.

"What office is he running for? Your friend, I mean?"

"Congress, Fifth District. Against somebody named Charles Portnoy. Have you heard of him?"

There was a long, long silence while Maggie's mind reeled. Even as they sat there, Ted was working on an analysis for Charles Portnoy's people, and if they liked it they would hire Maggie. For obvious reasons, she could not handle two candidates in the same race. If Peter Barnes had been more experienced, this would never have happened. Was there some way she could tell Peter Barnes to call back after Friday, so she could use this William Sutter as a fallback? The answer was no. She already knew—or would know—a lot about Portnoy's campaign just from the survey, whether he hired her or not. What she was thinking was unethical and immoral—in a profession that had never been known for its ethics or its morals. But Sutter was an ideal candidate—or so it seemed at this point. She would much rather work for Sutter, because it would be easier. She would rather not work against Sutter because it would be harder. She would rather work for Sutter, because she would see Peter Barnes again.

"I guess you haven't heard of Portnoy," Peter said. Maggie looked up to see him looking puzzled, obviously at her long pause.

She took a deep breath. "I've heard of him. He's a city supervisor, formerly sheriff, and I'm doing some work for him right now in my office. So I couldn't work for you even if you offered it to me. I'm afraid it was a wasted lunch for you."

"I'm sorry to hear that," Peter said. "But I don't think it was a wasted lunch. You seemed to enjoy it. I know I did."

Maggie tried to read some meaning into his words that went beyond politeness, and failed. She still couldn't find her shoe under the table, and that was beginning to fluster her more than anything about this failed lunch. The waiter returned with a little tray, and while Peter was busy adding on a tip and signing the form, Maggie ducked and took a hasty look under the table. There was no shoe in sight.

Peter stood up. "Ready?"

Maggie gulped, slid her other shoe off, and stood up, too. Perhaps, she thought, nobody would notice she was barefoot, whereas they certainly would notice her limping along on one green leather high heel. There was surely a shoe store nearby where she could buy something to put on her feet until she got home. She walked with as much dignity as she could muster across the room beside Peter. He was very tall and, barefoot, she felt dwarfed. Nobody seemed to be pointing and staring, and Peter did not seem to notice it, though there was a suspicious twinkle in his tawny eyes.

Just as they reached the maître d's desk, Maggie heard the voice of the waiter behind her: "Modom, oh modom, you left your shoes under the table."

Chapter Three

By Friday, Ted, happy as a clam, had wrung the Portnoy survey dry. Portnoy's likeliest voter was a woman between thirty and fifty, employed, some college, a reader of the afternoon paper, who watched three hours of TV daily, the news and sitcoms. The person least likely to vote for him was a member of the police department. He had ninety-percent name recognition among voters who had lived in San Francisco ten or more years. That was the good news. The bad news was that the average voter had only lived in the city for five years. The other bad-news side of the name-recognition factor was that it was due to the fact that, as sheriff, Portnoy had gone to his own jail, rather than carry out a court order. Some people thought him a dangerous radical for this, others thought he was heroic, and still others thought it was silly.

It was announced that William Sutter, of the old San Francisco family, partner in Sutter, Fenner, Mills, Markward and Peabody, had filed to be a candidate for Congress in the Fifth District. He had twelve years' experience in the law, belonged to all the right civic organizations and had chaired the Mayor's Task Force to Revitalize the Port of San Francisco, among other things.

This being San Francisco, on the same day two others filed: one on the vegetarian ticket, and one as an independent, running on the promise that if elected, he would dress as a panda bear while in Washington. He registered under the name of "None of the Above."

Maggie spent Friday morning working out a suggested strategy with Ted, who delivered it to the Portnoy offices that afternoon. An interminable weekend followed, and on Monday, about noon, Fred Oliver called and said they were on. Maggie had her first big campaign to run.

She soon forgot about Peter Barnes.

Except as a vague shadow standing behind the gigantic figure of William Sutter. The Sutter Tower, a television transmission facility, was nine-hundred-plus feet tall, and it dominated the city, standing as it did on Mount Sutter, itself more than nine hundred feet high. Aside from being eighteen hundred feet in the air and visible for a hundred miles, it was painted in red-and-white stripes and had flashing red lights on top. The man whose name it carried seemed to Maggie at least as visible, if not nearly as ugly. He either had no legislative record or a perfect legislative record—depending on the way you looked at it—he had a very photogenic family and a wife who worked at civic causes as hard as he did, and he had that damnable name. Charles Portnoy could not have a more formidable opponent. Maggie told him the first thing he had to do was raise twice as much money as he'd planned.

Maggie paid Ted the hundred she owed him and gave him a major raise. This did not make him any more respectful. She found herself working six, then seven, days a week. Her laundry began piling up at home, her cupboards went bare from lack of time to shop, she cut off all her friends and she got a cold. She decided success wasn't any fun.

She had a long talk with herself, took a day off, drank a lot of lemon tea and did six loads of laundry. She was just heading out the door to go to Petrini's Market when the phone rang. It could only be Ted, whom she had told not to call her unless Sutter died or the office burned to the ground.

"Well, which is it? Death or destruction?" she said as she answered the phone.

There was a pause on the other end, and then a puzzled vaguely familiar voice said, "Is this Maggie McGraw?"

For a moment Maggie considered telling whoever it was that they had the wrong number. "Uh, yes, it is," she muttered finally.

"Maggie, this is Peter Barnes."

Oh, no, thought Maggie. Why me, O Lord? He's calling to tell me how much he enjoyed watching me make a fool of myself. Before she could say anything he continued, "I've been very busy lately, and I meant to call sooner but couldn't."

"Mrrf," said Maggie.

"I was wondering if you'd like to go sailing this weekend."

Finding her voice at last, Maggie said, "Hmm."

"I'm sorry. I can't hear you. I think we have a bad connection. What did you say?"

"Yes." Maggie croaked. She meant yes, the connection was bad.

Peter Barnes must have misunderstood. "Good," he said. "I'll pick you up at eight on Saturday. Dress warmly, though I guess I don't need to tell you that. Now what's your address?"

"It's 250 Balboa, cross street Locust," Maggie said automatically, as she would to someone delivering something. Then she realized what she had said and began, "But—"

"Wonderful, see you then," Peter said and was gone before she could bring out another word.

What Maggie would have said, or should have said, was: I can't go sailing with you for about twenty reasons, one of them being that I am embarrassed about dropping my pearls in the sauce and leaving my stupid shoes under the stupid table, another of them being that I have spent considerable time *not* thinking about you. Not only that, I should be working on Saturday. But the really important reason is that we are on opposite sides of a political campaign and we shouldn't have anything to do with each other until after it's over, if then. And anyway, you are too good-looking and too rich for the likes of me.

And Maggie did say all this, to herself, all the way to Petrini's. Standing in front of the coffee and tea section, she announced aloud, "You're a fool if you go. It's not too late to call and say no." A Chinese couple beside her looked up from their silent equanimity and gave her a distinctly startled look.

But she didn't call back and say no, and when she went to the office the next day she did not say a word to Ted or to anyone else about going sailing on Saturday. It was probably the stupidest thing she'd ever done, she told herself. Well, maybe the weather would save her. Maybe Saturday would be one of those foggy days when not a boat ventured out on the bay. Or there would be ninety-mile-an-hour winds and the Coast Guard would put out small craft warnings.

By Saturday, Maggie had convinced herself that Peter Barnes had invited her to go sailing for a single reason: he wanted information on the Portnoy campaign. Why else would he invite her out after her performance at Rick's? Why else would he invite her out, period? Yalies with sailboats didn't invite Irish pols' daughters anywhere. Wasn't there even a novel about that? Maggie was certain that Peter Barnes was up to no good at all. Remember Jim, she told herself.

Saturday dawned bright and beautiful, a perfect sailing day. Maggie could not see a wisp of fog on the horizon, and she was torn between being happy and being disappointed. She pulled on her worst jeans, a turtleneck and her deck shoes and made a bundle of two more sweaters. She had sailed enough to know that even on the hottest day sailing on the Bay was a cold business.

She was waiting with a thermos of hot coffee, and when Peter rang her bell at the entrance downstairs, instead of buzzing him in, she took off down the three flights of carpeted stairs. She did not want him to catch a glimpse of the chaos that the Portnoy campaign had made of her apartment. Or of any of the papers that made up the chaos.

She was a little surprised at his car, a small Japanese something or other, but not at his dress, which was similar to hers: jeans, turtleneck and a terrible sweatshirt that seemed to have once said Martha's Vineyard but was too old and faded for her to really tell. He looked just as good as he had in his three-piece suit at lunch, Maggie thought. Maybe better.

He, however, was delighted to see her thermos of coffee and skillfully drove one-handed and drank a cup as they took the tunnel under the Presidio and came out on the approaches to the Golden Gate Bridge. His boat, he explained, was berthed in Sausalito, on the other side. Maggie was grateful for the fact that the conversation was limited to the view and the weather.

She was also surprised by his boat when they walked out on the dock carrying what seemed like a ton of equipment. Maggie remembered *Westwind II* from the picture, but this wasn't it. This was a much smaller boat, a single-masted sloop, very sleek and trim in black and gold and white with black sail covers. Lettered on its elegant white transom was the name *Maria*.

Maggie knew what to do without being told. She put on her life jacket, stowed everything aboard the boat and began taking the covers off the sails. She took charge of the jib, the smaller sail in front, carefully attaching each of the metal snaps to the stay, the heavy wire that ran from the bow up to the top of the mast. She felt very proud of herself. It had been three years since she'd sailed, and she still remembered how to do this.

Since there wasn't any wind yet, no sails went up. Peter started the motor and signaled to Maggie to take the tiller. Then they were slowly moving through a cool, hazy water-world toward the distant silver towers of the city. Beside them the stylish little houses of Sausalito spilled down the steep hills to the water. Only the tiniest of waves lapped at the bow of the boat. A few other boats were out, sails up and luffing a bit, waiting for the wind. Two or three powerboats roared past, rocking everything in their wake, and in the distance a monstrous container ship, loaded to the gunwales, glided under the Golden Gate Bridge.

Peter turned off the motor and hoisted the mainsail. It flapped feebly, the sound barely audible above the slap of the water on the hull. Now all there was to do was wait for the rising wind. And talk. This, Maggie guessed would be the moment he would start asking about the Portnoy campaign. She checked the distance to shore—half a mile perhaps—and estimated that she could swim it, should he try to hold her hostage to get information.

"You've sailed before, haven't you?" Peter asked pleasantly.

Maggie had an answer ready. "It's none of—" she said before she realized what he had said, and made a quick amendment. "I mean, it's *one* of my favorite things to do, except that I never have time. And I don't have a sailboat, so I have to go with friends who do, and right now I don't know anyone who has a boat."

"Except me." Peter Barnes grinned, showing those straight white teeth and squinting at her under those dark brows. She could see him getting more tanned, even in the gentle rays of the morning sun. Maggie would come home from a day on the Bay with a sunburn and more freckles.

"Have you been sailing long?" Maggie asked, sure she knew the answer.

"Most of my life." That was the answer she'd expected.

"How old were you when you got your first boat?"

"Uh, thirty-five." He seemed startled at the question.

Maggie gaped. That was *not* the answer she'd expected. She figured his father had probably given him his first day sailer at age ten or something.

She had hold of the tiller, though there was nothing to do with it, since there was no wind. Peter was lolling in the sun, his feet stretched out across the boat.

"This is my first boat. I bought it here."

"What about *Westwind II*?" Maggie blurted before she could stop herself.

"How do you know *Westwind II*?" Peter asked, clearly surprised.

Maggie could think of nothing to do but confess. "When Ted and I were looking at your files to find out who they belonged to, there was a picture of you in there in front of *Westwind II*. I put it together with Yale and some kind of inheritance and figured . . ."

"Figured I was born with a silver sailboat in my mouth, right?"

Maggie's face felt as fiery as her hair. "Yes."

"Well, I guess I don't blame you. Here, put the tiller over." He put his hand over hers to make a minor adjustment. His brown fingers engulfed her small white ones, and Maggie found herself wishing he would not take his hand away. But it was gone in an instant.

"I guess I'd better explain. I'm not what you think I am," he continued. "I guess I'm not what I think I am, for that matter. But here's the story of my life, in twenty-five words or less."

"I didn't think a lawyer could do anything in twenty-five words or less," Maggie said seriously.

"Sure they can." He grinned. "When they aren't getting paid for it. Anyhow, here are the twenty-five words: grew up in Newport, Rhode Island, father sold insurance, mother a housewife, middle-class, Yale on a scholarship, clerked for a judge for a year, worked for a big firm in New York City for ten years, moved here."

"That was about forty words," Maggie insisted. She had been counting on her fingers.

A puff of wind rattled the sail, and they both looked up.

"False alarm," Peter said. "What else do you want to know? What did I leave out of my deposition? Before you, my life is an open book." He made a grand bowing gesture, and the boat rocked. Maggie felt slightly dizzy—from the motion of the boat, of course.

"How did you learn to sail?" Maggie asked.

"Do you know anything about Newport?"

Maggie shook her head.

"Mansions, the Navy, tennis and yachting. The America's Cup, until it went to Australia, was always at Newport. So I had a lot of friends who had boats, being almost the only non-rich, non-Navy kid around. And naturally I learned how to sail. I grew up wanting to crew in the America's Cup, but I didn't have the time or the money to do that."

"So how—" Maggie began.

"So how did I get the money to buy this one? Hard work. I did have an inheritance, though. After law school I clerked a year for a federal judge. My inheritance came when he died: he left me his law library. I went to work for a New York law firm. I made good money, but I really didn't like what I was doing, and I hated New York. Everybody's in such a charged-up state, so frantic. And, more important, it's right on the Atlantic Ocean but there's no feel of the sea to it at all. Just that dirty river.

"Two years ago I came out here on vacation and went to see one of my Yale classmates, Bill Sutter. I sat in his office and looked out and I could see sailboats, and I must have looked so green with envy that Bill offered me a partnership. Now I'm not making nearly as much money—I'm a junior partner again—but I can look out my office window and see sailboats. And it's a small firm, unlike the New York firm, which had over a hundred partners. I can do what I please."

Maggie started to say, "And what's that?" Then she heard the sail snap as if filled.

"Wind's up." Peter jumped up and reached for the jib. Maggie adjusted the tiller to catch all the wind and was watching the mainsail fill when she heard the squealing that meant the jib was being hoisted. Then she heard a burst of laughter from Peter, and more laughter carried by the wind from a nearby boat, and she glanced over to see what was so funny.

The triangular sail, which she had so neatly snapped on its wire, was neatly snapped on upside down. The worst landlubber could see that something was badly wrong with beautiful little *Maria*. They were probably laughing up there on the Golden Gate Bridge, Maggie thought. She slid down in the boat as far as she could.

After Peter had quickly put the sail right, politely acting as if anybody could have put the jib on upside down, they sailed *Maria* as if she were an America's Cup competitor. Or Peter did. All Maggie could do was hold on for dear life and follow his orders.

With the wind, which was cold, came waves, and with the waves came spray, and Maggie and Peter each struggled into a set of yellow foul-weather gear he kept in the cockpit. They tacked out under the Golden Gate Bridge and beyond, to the open sea, where only the best and the bravest went, and came back with the wind behind them, almost running free. Maggie kept the tiller and Peter worked the sails. It was, Maggie thought, an indescribable feeling, especially on the long, glorious run up to Angel Island. It was the wind in your hair and the cold salt spray on your face, the hum of the rigging, the cry of "Hard alee" before the helm went over, the smooth bellying of the sails, the sleek little boat heeling over, sometimes at impossible angles, the smell of the salt sea, the hiss of the water past the hull, the look of the choppy, foaming green-and-white water. It was here and now, being alive at every moment, aware that you were taming hostile water and dangerous wind in a frail craft of wood, fiberglass and canvas.

When they were safely anchored at Angel Island, Maggie was cold, wet and tired and her hands hurt from pulling on wet ropes. Her muscles were sore, and she was shaking a bit from the primordial fear of the cold, dark water less than an inch away, the treacherous wind that could veer and capsize a small boat and the tides that could carry the *Maria* out into the trackless, icy North Pacific faster than she could sail or motor back.

So Maggie said, "I never had so much fun in my life!" She sprawled, exhausted, against the side, still in her foul-weather gear.

"You're pretty handy around a boat," Peter said. "As good a crew as I ever had." He, on the other hand, was stripping off his yellow rain gear.

Maggie suddenly sobered. "You are a terrific liar. I put the jib on upside down."

"Well, there's that." He grinned. "Common mistake. I've seen it done in the America's Cup. You're going to get broiled if you don't get out of that gear."

"I noticed the same thing myself," Maggie said, realizing that she now felt as if she were inside a steam bath. She stood up and began to struggle out of her jacket. Her legs felt rubbery.

Maria was one of a number of boats moored in the lee of Angel Island, in a sheltered cove. Wooded, green Angel Island, the largest in the Bay, lay not far from rocky little Alcatraz, with its grim, decaying prison blocks. Fittingly, at Alcatraz there was no shelter for boats, only treacherous rocks.

By now a noontime sun beat down from a cloudless sky. There was not a breath of wind in the lee of the island. Voices and laughter floated across the shimmering water from boats moored nearby. It seemed an entirely different world from that of wind and spray and crackling sails a few hundred yards away.

While Maggie shed as many layers of clothes as seemed decent, Peter brought out the cooler he had lugged from the car. He pulled out turkey sandwiches with lettuce, onion, tomato, mayonnaise and mustard on sourdough rolls, pickles, olives, a container of potato salad, soft drinks, beer and a bottle of Chablis. From within the cockpit came napkins, silver, a corkscrew and two wineglasses. All of this he laid out buffet-style on the ledge above the cockpit. Then he turned to Maggie and said, "Modom, your pleasure?"

"I think I'll have a turkey sandwich and some potato salad," Maggie said ingenuously. She walked the length of the well of the gently rocking boat in three steps.

"And I think I'll have the same. I took a chance you liked turkey. A glass of wine?" As he spoke, he opened the bottle, then poured two glasses.

He handed Maggie hers, and as they stood there, he towering over her, he looked deeply and meaningfully into her eyes and clinked his glass against hers. "May your jib always be right side up."

The chill, dry white wine slid down her throat like silk, hit her famished stomach and, leaving only a warm spot, immediately U-turned and went straight to her head. It felt so deliciously light and muzzy that she took another big swallow and immediately realized how beautiful, and how funny the world really was. She shot a glance over at the bottle, wondering what special ingredient the wine contained, but it seemed to be plain old wine with a familiar label. Smiling, she grabbed a sandwich and, ducking under the boom, went to sit beside Peter, who seemed to be watching her with some interest. His long legs went almost all the way across the boat.

Maggie studied him out of the corner of her eye. His profile was as good as the rest of him. His nose was a bit hawkish under his dark brows, his mouth was thin and wide, and his blond hair looked even better windblown. As for the rest, Maggie could—and, somewhat to her surprise, did—imagine what it looked like under the clothes. Long and lean and well-muscled, but not too well. And tanned. A difficult thing to achieve in San Francisco, a tan, but he had a beautiful one.

"How do you stay so tan?" Maggie asked before she could stop herself.

"What if I said I went to a tanning parlor?" he asked.

Maggie looked at him closely. She shook her head. "I wouldn't believe you. You're not the type."

She immediately wished she hadn't said that, because he responded with the inevitable question: "What type am I, then?"

Peter Barnes seemed to be a set of contradictions, she thought. Very polite, a bit laconic, perhaps even shy. He seemed unaware of his good looks. He had an eastern uptightness combined with a California laid-backness. It confused her. She had been so sure of the reason he had invited her sailing today, and it had proved to be wrong. She decided that evasion of the question was the better part of valor.

Maria had swung around so that they were facing the great mass of Angel Island. Some ruined buildings were barely visible through the gigantic old eucalyptus trees.

Maggie munched on her sandwich and said, her words somewhat muffled by the sourdough, "My grandparents used to live there."

"Really? I thought it was uninhabited."

"It is now. Now it's a state park, but it used to be used for a lot of things—military post, immigration station, quarantine station."

"Why did your grandparents live here?"

Maggie took another sip of wine. The food seemed to be clearing her head but leaving the warm glow. "Grandpa was an army officer. But that's not the best part of the story. The part I like is that my grandmother used to take the army launch over to Alcatraz to play bridge with the warden's wife.''

"Wow," said Peter, looking impressed.

"May I have some more of that wine?" Maggie held out her glass.

"Sure." Peter reached for the bottle. "So do you come from an old army family?"

"No, not that I know of. Grandpa was the exception. My father was a fireman, or he started out that way, anyway. Then he went into politics. An old-time Irish pol."

"So you come by your profession honestly." Peter grinned that dazzling grin. "What did he do in politics?"

Peter filled her glass again, and put down the bottle, and when next Maggie noticed, his arm was behind her shoulders. It felt very nice, she thought.

She finished the sandwich and some potato salad and washed it down with another swig of wine. "He was a city supervisor for years, and then he had various jobs around city hall. Depending on who was mayor, of course. Things were different then. But I did kind of grow up in a smoke-filled room."

"Was that fun?"

The boat had swung again, and Maggie was now staring out at a vast expanse of water and a tanker making its way out from the refineries at the north end of the Bay. Its progress was hypnotically slow. Maggie watched, fascinated.

"Ahem," Peter said beside her.

"I'm sorry," Maggie told him. "I didn't hear what you said."

"I asked if it was fun, growing up in a smoke-filled room."

Maggie turned and looked him straight in the eye. "The only thing more fun than that is running before the wind in a sailboat." Then she took a last swallow of her wine, put the glass down and said, "Do you mind if I just lie down here on the deck for a few minutes?"

Without waiting for an answer, she put a life jacket under her head and stretched out on her back. She wasn't really sleepy, she was just functioning too slowly to both sit up and think at the same time. She closed her eyes tight but still could see the sun through her eyelids.

"Do you use anything you learned in that smoke-filled room now?"

"Sure," Maggie said contentedly. "There are certain rules that were invented in ancient Greece, probably."

"Like what?"

"Like never get defensive. Always start out on the positive. Run on your record if it's good, run on your opponent's if it's bad." Through the warm, relaxed body ran a small alarm bell of tension.

"What do you think about negative campaigns?"

"Smear jobs, you mean? I think they're counter-productive, but I'm not the campaign manager." Maggie suddenly sat up. "Is your next question 'What's the strategy for Charles Portnoy?' Is that why you brought me out here? A little industrial espionage on behalf of your friend Mr. Sutter? Take her out on a boat and give her some wine and she'll tell all?

People who look and act like you do don't take out people who look and act like I do unless they have some nefarious reason."

Peter sat up straight. "You've got it all wrong, Maggie—"

She wouldn't let him finish. "No, I don't have it wrong. Can you get this bucket over to that old dock over there, or do I have to swim?"

And that was how Maggie ended up walking across Angel Island to Hospital Cove and taking the ferry and then the bus home on the day she had the most fun in her life.

Afterward, she had only one regret: that she hadn't asked him who Maria was.

Chapter Four

Peter was astounded by Maggie's response to his question. Her reactions showed how political an animal she really was. It had never crossed his mind that she might think he was after information. In his experience, he mused, women generally thought he was after something else. He sat in the boat a long time, thinking, and then he took it in to the dock and drove home thinking, and then he had a long Scotch and water and thought some more.

And what he thought was this: all his life he'd had a low opinion of people in politics, and so when Bill Sutter had told him that he was considering running for the vacant congressional seat, Peter had advised him not to do it. But Bill Sutter had politics in his genes, and when he'd asked for help, Peter had agreed to give it. Within limitations. Something easy, something behind the scenes, something that wouldn't take much time, since he now had the Rincon Oil acquisition on his hands. Bill had agreed that Rincon Oil was important to the firm and agreed that Peter should be involved as little as possible in the campaign. Moral support, he'd said.

It was really just one more complication in a life that he was trying to uncomplicate. One more problem to wind down before he took off. But he couldn't turn Bill down.

The other complication that he had managed to uncomplicate, deliberately, was his relationship with the opposite sex. In New York he'd sometimes found himself juggling two or three at a time. Beautiful, brittle women with designer clothes who talked about whoever was on the cover of *Vanity Fair* that month. He'd gotten serious about one or two—an editor at an art house, a medical student—real people, but they, too, had looked at him, appalled, when they'd learned that he planned one day to give up being a yuppie lawyer and do what he was going to do. Oh, all of them thought it was terrific at first, and then they learned what it entailed and changed their minds. Childish, irresponsible, bad marriage material, he was. If he'd do that, what else would he do? they must have asked themselves.

Moving to San Francisco had uncomplicated that situation. And he'd planned to leave it uncomplicated while he uncomplicated everything else, and then he'd be ready to go. But along came this little redheaded freckled feisty kid, by accident, with the improbable name of Maggie McGraw, with the most improbable job he'd ever heard of, and he'd taken one look and the roof had fallen in on him. It was truly absurd, he thought. He couldn't really figure out what had attracted him. She was not beautiful by any means, but those big green eyes under the flyaway red hair, in that little-girl face—and the freckles—brought out all his protective instincts. But she obviously didn't need protection, either. She was as independent and proud as a hog on ice, as his mother would have said. She had an endearingly klutzy quality and, as he had just learned, she possessed a blistering honesty. All qualities he valued, but none of them enough to cause him to go into a tailspin. All he could attribute it to was a concept that he certainly did not believe in: love at first sight.

Before he could stop himself, he'd talked Bill Sutter into letting him interview Maggie about working on the campaign. And then he'd talked to himself for a while about all the reasons he shouldn't get entangled with anyone right now, and then he'd invited her sailing anyway. She knew a little about sailing, and that was a plus. But the rest of it was all minuses. She'd misread him as completely as he'd misread her. She was the only person, he guessed, who had ever walked home from a date on a sailboat in the middle of San Francisco Bay. He smiled, then frowned.

Peter finished his Scotch and said, ''Barnes, as of today you stay away from Maggie McGraw. It's reckless endangerment. Take cold showers.''

The following day, Sunday, Maggie's phone rang at least ten times. She refused to answer.

On Monday, back in the office, sunburned from
sailing, Maggie wrote a mailer for Carol Gold, showing her in action as president of the League of Woman
Voters and as the chairman of a committee that had
gotten a proposition on the ballot to stem the tide of
"Manhattanization"—the wall of high rises that was
going up downtown. Based on the results of a quick
and dirty—because that was all she could afford—
telephone survey, Maggie advised Carol to sharpen her
positions on the home-porting of the battleship Mis-
souri in San Francisco, the Candlestick Park contro-
versy and tearing down the Embarcadero Freeway.
Maggie was glad *she* didn't have to have positions on
these issues—they were painful and very compli-
cated—but they were what the voting public was concerned about.

She told Ted that she would accept no phone calls
from Peter Barnes, or anyone else with the Sutter
Campaign. Ted looked at her oddly and then asked
her where she'd gotten such a terrible sunburn. "On
the roof of my apartment building," she snapped.
"Can't you find anything to do besides ask nosy
questions?"

There were two or three calls that Ted answered that
might have been Peter Barnes—Maggie didn't ask,
and Ted didn't volunteer the information.

Maggie bought an answering machine on her lunch
hour and hooked it up when she got home. She refused to listen to any of the messages left.

On Tuesday, no calls came, but a telegram was delivered. Ted exhibited much curiosity, but Maggie
managed to hide if from him. It read: Call me this

morning or else. Maggie ignored it. She was not afraid of anything Peter Barnes could threaten her with.

Immediately thereafter, Charles Portnoy came lumbering into her office. Maggie liked him a lot, and would have wanted him to win even if she hadn't been being paid to help him. He was a big, shaggy man who had started out in a career in law enforcement and had gotten himself a night school education. He'd run for sheriff and won, and had then astonished everyone with his unconventional views. Ordered by the court to evict some old men from a hotel so that it could be torn down, he had refused to give the order and been locked up in his own jail. In any other city that would have doomed him, but this was San Francisco. He had been president of the board of supervisors for some years. He was still unconventional, brilliant and ahead of his time. He was not an easy commodity to package and market, either, Maggie thought.

"The survey says that if the vote was today it would be Sutter eighteen percent, Portnoy fifteen percent and the rest—"

"The rest are for 'None of the Above,' right?" Portnoy said, sitting on a folding chair that looked like a toy under him. "I don't blame them. I'll vote for him myself."

"Actually, the way we asked the question was: 'If you were voting today, who would you vote for in your congressional district race?' That means the rest didn't know who they were going to vote for, because they didn't know who was running. When we asked it another way, naming the candidates, you got twenty percent, Sutter got thirty and roughly fifty percent were undecided. It isn't as bad as I thought it would be, but it isn't good. Nobody's started campaigning yet."

"We need more money, don't we?"

"Every bit would help."

"Sutter's having a dinner at the Olympic Club next week—two hundred and fifty dollars a head. I'm having a twenty-dollar-a-head fried chicken picnic in the park. I'll bet it gets more money in than he does."

Maggie looked impressed. "You don't need a campaign consultant."

At that very moment, the door to the office burst open and a delivery man came staggering in under the weight of the largest collection of flowers Maggie had ever seen. Portnoy and Maggie stared. There were roses, daffodils, birds of paradise, chrysanthemums, red, white, blue, purple, orange and yellow flowers, all shooting out like a fireworks display.

"We don't have any winning racehorses," Ted said. "Bay Meadows is way south of here."

"There must be some mistake," Maggie gasped.

"I was told to deliver these to Maggie McGraw at this address," said the confused delivery man.

Charles Portnoy was laughing.

"Put them over there by the window," Maggie said resignedly. "Ted, clear off a place."

They took up an entire table. The tiny card read Call me, your secret admirer. Unfortunately, Ted found it first, hidden among the daffodils. He read it out loud.

"Let's get back to work," Maggie said.

"Aren't you going to call him?" asked Ted.

* * *

The following day, during an important strategy meeting attended by Fred Oliver, Portnoy's campaign manager, and four outside consultants, a clown walked into the office and filled it with helium balloons in a rainbow of colors all of which had the same message printed on them: Call me now: 555-9919.

"One ninety-eight, one ninety-nine, two hundred," Ted said, batting his way through. "More or less."

The balloons nudged each other just below the ceiling like nursing kittens.

There was an awed silence in the room.

Maggie stood up. "I'll use the pay phone in the lobby," she said, grabbing a red balloon to refer to the number.

Having forgotten her purse, Maggie had to borrow two dimes from the semimoribund security guard in the lobby. And she had forgotten how open the phone was. Therefore, when Peter Barnes answered the phone, she kept her voice to a harsh whisper. "Now I've called. Will you stop?"

"We have to talk, Maggie. How about dinner tonight?"

"We do *not* have to talk. No dinner."

"Why are you whispering?"

"Because about fifty people can hear me."

"Why no dinner?"

"Because I don't want to have anything to do with you, you spy."

"Maggie, use your head. I'm not spying. I want to see you."

"I don't want to see you. And I *can't* be seen with you. You're the enemy, even if you aren't spying, which I doubt."

"Okay, we'll go someplace where we can't be seen."

"The deep dark woods?" Maggie said, sarcastically, though she felt her resolve fading.

"How about your place?"

"No!" Maggie almost yelped, thinking of Portnoy's papers spread all over the place.

"What about mine?"

"That's even worse," Maggie said.

"Can you think of somewhere else where we wouldn't be seen? Rick's? Under the Ferry building clock? Ocean Beach at dawn?"

"What will you do if I don't meet you?"

"Flowers, balloons were only the beginning. There are those streamers they tow behind biplanes, and—"

"Okay, I'll be at your apartment tonight at eight."

"It's 8000 Vallejo, number 10."

She carefully wrote the address on the balloon, having nothing else to write on. Just as she completed the *j* there was a loud explosion and the balloon disappeared.

The four or five people passing through the lobby had frozen in their tracks. The security guard had lumbered to his feet and had his hand on his nightstick.

"What was that?" Peter could be heard saying from the receiver that Maggie had dropped in surprise.

Peter Barnes's apartment building was in the Spanish mission style popular in the twenties. It was white stucco, with elaborate black wrought-iron window grills and a red tile roof, and was nestled up against one of the steepest hills in the city. A street was not really considered steep unless its accompanying sidewalk had steps in it. This one, the one Maggie was puffing up now, had steps—two blocks of them just to reach Vallejo Street.

Maggie had decided to forgo the pleasures of a taxi and take the bus. Since the bus couldn't get up the hill, Maggie had no choice but to pick her long, weary way up. She therefore arrived at the arched door of 8000 Vallejo puffing and hot, though the usual evening chill had fallen over the city.

She pushed the white porcelain button marked 10 in the brass plate that listed the apartments within.

"Maggie?" said the intercom.

"Yes."

The door lock buzzed, and from long experience Maggie leaped for it and got the door open before it stopped and locked her out again. Inside she found herself in a red-carpeted lobby with a winding staircase rising from the center. Lush green plants lined the walls. So handsome were they that Maggie checked to be sure they weren't plastic.

Two flights later, she was standing openmouthed in Peter's apartment. The apartment was nice enough, but that was not what startled Maggie. It was the view, from Peter's window. Over the low rooftops of the Marina district below, you could see everything from the Golden Gate Bridge to Coit Tower—in short, everything worth seeing on the Bay.

"Wow," she said, awed. "You can see sailboats from work, and sailboats at home."

"That's right," he said. "When you see the bathroom and kitchen, you'll understand what I gave up for that view."

"The original plumbing and fixtures, I'll bet," Maggie said.

"You've been here before," he said.

Maggie shook her head. "Naw. I know San Franciscans are the only people in the world who would rather have a view than a kitchen."

He took Maggie's coat and led her to a seat on the big, soft sofa. "What would you like to drink?"

"Nothing, thank you." Maggie suddenly remembered what she was here for and why she was angry at Peter.

"I think for this evening's purposes you should have one. Do you like Scotch?"

Maggie didn't care one way of the other about Scotch. She decided to accept the drink, since he seemed bent on it.

While he was in the kitchen fixing the drinks, Maggie looked around the room. The furniture was good, but there wasn't much of it. There was a fine Persian rug on the floor, and there was a fireplace with an ample supply of logs. Above the fireplace was an oil painting of a tall ship under sail, and the wall opposite was full of books. In one corner was a large globe in a stand, and on one wall was a huge map of the world.

Maggie stood up and walked over to read the titles of the books. She always considered this an excellent insight into the character of the books' owner. She was not surprised to see that many of them were about sailing, that there was a shelf that consisted of every great sea novel she had ever heard of—*Moby Dick*, the *Bounty* Trilogy, Joseph Conrad, Jack London, the Hornblower series. There were the great explorations—*Hakluyt's Voyages, The Journals of Captain Cook*. And there were more: books about Polynesia, Australia, Singapore, the Skeleton Coast, Reunion Island, the West Indies, Baja California. He had books on everything from botany to politics.

She was still standing in front of the books when he came back into the room carrying two glasses. He handed Maggie one.

"You've got quite a collection here." She nodded at the books.

"Thirty years' worth," he said.

"They are all about sailing or South Sea islands. Are you planning a trip?"

"All my life. When I was ten I decided I wanted to do two things—crew in the America's Cup, and sail around the world. I couldn't do the first, but I'm still going to do the second."

His tawny eyes had a faraway expression in them as if he were already in the South Seas. Maggie felt a wave of longing for places named Tahiti and Tongareva, a flash of a terrible desire to sail around the world.

"I've been charting my course for twenty-five years, too." He took her elbow and led her toward the gigantic world map. "Here's the latest one: San Francisco direct to the Marquesas, then the Societies, the

Cooks, Samoa, Fiji, down to New Zealand— Are you okay?" He looked down at Maggie in concern.

She knew her face was bright red, and it took an effort not to blurt out, "Oh, please take me, please."

Instead she said, "It's the Scotch. It always makes me turn red." Suddenly she wanted to leave, to end this pain. This man was the enemy, he had blackmailed her into coming to his apartment, and now he was torturing her with talk of sailing to fabled islands. She added, "Let's get this over with. Why do you want to talk to me?"

She thought he looked disappointed, but he immediately changed the subject. "Okay, we'll do it your way. I want you to know I wasn't trying to get information out of you the other day, Maggie. You've got to believe me."

"Why? Why should I believe you?"

"First of all, you should realize that I'm an attorney, and if I wanted to get information out of you I would have framed my questions better. You wouldn't have even known I got it. But the real reason you should believe me is that I'm not like that— I'm not sneaky. I'm a truthful person."

He was easing her toward the couch, Maggie noticed. Well, she wouldn't sit down.

"If you are a truthful person, then tell me why you invited me sailing."

That seemed to give him pause. "That's a strange question," he said at last. "Why does any man ask a woman anywhere? Because I was—am—attracted to you. Because you're terrific-looking and because you're bright and because you lose your shoes under the table. Because I wanted to get to know you better. Because I thought you looked like you liked to sail. Is that good enough?''

Maggie discovered that she was sitting on the couch and that Peter was beside her. His last remark had made her go weak in the knees.

"It had nothing to do with my working for Charles Portnoy?"

"Scout's honor," he said, holding up one hand. "I didn't even think about it. I try not to think about Bill Sutter's campaign, too. Most especially when I'm out on the boat."

"And you don't care if I lose my shoes or put the jib up wrong?" Maggie could still hardly believe it.

"Part of your charm." His arm was around her shoulders again.

"I have freckles, you know," she said idiotically.

"So I see." He bent his head toward hers and looked long and deep into her eyes.

There was a long, low drumming sound, and a pale flash hurtled around the corner from the hall, shot across the living room and hurled itself onto the couch between Maggie and Peter. Maggie jumped and found herself looking into the beautiful blue eyes of the largest Siamese cat she had ever seen.

"This is Genghis Khat," Peter said. "I thought I had him locked up."

"Purrrr," said Genghis Khat.

"He probably broke the door down," Maggie suggested.

"Or used a key," Peter said. "Besides weighing twenty pounds, he's smart for a cat. Here, big guy, back to your room." He started to pick the cat up.

But Maggie stopped him. "No, no, he's fine. Leave him." If it hadn't been for Genghis Khat, she figured, things would have developed much faster in this relationship than she wanted. It was probably a good thing to have a smart twenty-pound cat in between them. She scratched Genghis Khat behind the ears and was rewarded with a louder "Purrrr."

"So, are we friends?" Peter asked.

"I guess so, but there are conditions."

"Such as?"

"Well, mainly we can't be seen together. You have to understand that it would be considered treason."

"Shot at dawn, last cigarette, do you want a blindfold? That kind of treason?"

"Yep."

"I can live with that."

"It's not as easy as you think. There are only about seven hundred thousand people in San Francisco. It's a very small town."

Peter laughed, disturbing the cat, who gave him a distinctly dirty look. "We can go sailing—that's safe—and we can go out of town."

"There are lots of places to go out of town, and they're all full of San Francisco people getting out of town."

"Isn't there someplace San Francisco people don't go?"

"Yeah, Los Angeles, at least not if they can help it."

"Wanna go to L.A.?" Peter said lasciviously.

"No!" Maggie got a dirty look herself from the cat. "I went there once, and I didn't like it."

"How long were you there?"

"Two hours. It was a layover at the airport."

"I see," said Peter, pulling on his chin wisely.

"So, anyway, the first condition is that we can't be seen together, and the second is that we never, never, discuss the campaign or the candidates or anything even distantly related."

"That one should be very easy. I'm already sick of it."

Maggie had a third condition. *Take me on that round-the-world sail.* But she bit her tongue.

In the end, they agreed to go sailing again the following Saturday, weather permitting. Weather not permitting, Maggie was to think of a safe place to go out of town. Peter had no requirements in that regard, as long as it was interesting.

He was surprised to learn that Maggie had no car, and he drove her home. They sealed their bargain with a solemn handshake, no more, at the door. Maggie went upstairs to her apartment and spent the rest of the evening singing happily to herself and picking cat hair off her black wool skirt.

Chapter Five

Peter, on the other hand, was less happy, not with Maggie, but with himself. He was expending a lot of emotional capital on what his head told him would be another hopeless case. He was going to get burned. But he couldn't seem to help himself. She hadn't really batted an eyelash about sailing around the world, and that reaction was exceptional. Most women blurted out, "Oh, I want to go, take me." Only later, when they found out that it wouldn't be like a world cruise on the QEII, that he planned to take years, that there wouldn't be a hot-water heater aboard, did they change their minds and decide he was off his rocker.

Maggie's only reaction was to blush, or something, from the Scotch, she said. He knew that wasn't true.

Then and there, he'd gotten this crazy idea in his head to ask her to go along. He'd never before run across anyone that he thought he could stand to be with for years on a small boat, so he'd always planned it solo. And, though it was always the great adventure, everyone's wildest dream, the truth of it was that it wasn't all South Sea islands and warm sun. He'd been on some long ocean sails, and he knew it was a lot like the airline pilot's description of flying: hundreds of hours of crushing boredom, a few seconds of pure terror. Long watches had to be stood; the food went from bad to horrible, things you couldn't live without broke, and you lived without them; you washed everything, including yourself, in cold salt water. There was no newspaper, no TV, no movies; you could only take a few books. You could run into a typhoon, you could get lost, you could run out of water, you could get sick. The only thing worse than getting sick a thousand miles from the nearest land was getting sick in New Guinea.

And then there was Maggie herself, obviously working at something she loved, even though he didn't understand why she loved it. But she obviously loved sailing, too. On the Bay. The only place she'd sailed. All she would know was sailing all day and then having a terrific dinner in Sausalito, and then going home to a long, hot shower and her own snug bed. No, Maggie was not likely to want to take on a few years of misery just for a month or two in Pago Pago. She was a woman on the way up, soon to be a smashing success. Politics was in her genes, too. It was a hereditary disability. You couldn't expect her to drop everything and live someone else's dream.

"Well, Genghis," he said to the cat in his lap, "do you like her? I do, too, and I don't know what to do about it."

The balloons stayed on the ceiling the rest of the week, though occasionally one would lose helium and begin to sink to the floor. Ted would then stalk them with a pin that he kept on his desk for that purpose. He did this gleefully, and every time he popped one Maggie jumped and yelled at him. The flowers began to wilt, and Maggie threw them out as soon as they even started to look unhealthy. By week's end, the flower arrangement looked like a picked-over corn-field. Every hour or so Ted would ask, "Who's your secret admirer?" and Maggie would shake her head and say, "Nobody."

But very little got past Ted. "Maggie," he said, looking up from his computer printouts, "you are really acting weird lately."

Maggie looked down her nose at him and said, "I beg your pardon?" in as chilly a tone as she could muster. She was secretly relieved at the timing of this statement. They were alone together in the office. Usually Ted said things like that in front of three or four other people.

"Do you realize you are going around humming? And tunelessly, I might add. It would be better if you hummed something specific. Plus, you've got this really dumb grin all the time, *and* you keep putting your hand on your chest and taking a deep breath. I'm not a doctor, but even I can tell something is wrong. Frankly, I think it's a psychiatric problem."

"Ted," Maggie said sweetly, "go soak your head."

On the other hand, things were beginning to mesh on the campaigns. Poor, nervous Harley Davis got a terrific telephone survey, putting him way ahead of the opposition. Carol Gold had been invited to debate the home-porting issue on local television, which would give her all kinds of exposure. And Charles Portnoy was showing an astonishing ability to attract campaign contributions. All in all, Maggie thought, it had been a pretty good week, if you discounted the flowers and the balloons. Especially the damned balloons. And her heart fluttered once again to think that in less than twenty-four hours she would be seeing her secret admirer again. He really was secret, too, she thought . . . and thought and thought.

"Maggie, cut it out. I can't stand the humming."

But this Saturday did not dawn as well as the last. It was foggy and overcast. The fog was expected to clear by midmorning, but it was expected to be cleared by high winds with gusts up to fifty miles an hour. That meant sailing was out.

So Maggie fell back on the elephant seals.

To her glee, Peter had never heard of them. Elephant seals were always so much more fun if they were a surprise. Or perhaps "shock" was the word.

By the time they reached Año Nuevo Point, some forty miles south of San Francisco on the spectacular—and sometimes terrifying—coastal highway, the fog was gone.

As they pulled into the parking lot of the state reserve—the elephant seals were a protected species—Maggie delivered a short history.

"Until fifty years ago, they were thought to be extinct. The whalers in the 1800s got them all for their blubber. But then a few of them were sighted on an island off Baja California. They were protected by law and they multiplied. Now they hang around all the way up the coast."

Peter was busy getting a blue parka out of the trunk of the car. The wind was blowing fiercely.

"Are they friendly?" he asked, pulling on the parka and turning up the collar.

Maggie laughed. "I don't think you'd want a friendly elephant seal around." She was already bundled up in a parka and a knit cap, standing and watching him with her hands in her pockets. He looked heartrendingly gorgeous, even in the wind, which, Maggie mused, probably didn't bother him a bit. Wind to a sailor was life. He hung a pair of binoculars around his neck and, holding out a hand, said, "Let's go."

Maggie took his hand and pointed out the beginning of the trail. It was a little over a mile to the end of the point, on a winding path through head-high yellow blooming lupine. Every few feet, Maggie was compelled to stop and sniff its intoxicating smell. There were other people on the trail, but far enough away that Maggie still felt she and Peter were alone.

Maggie had a little trouble with the huge sand dune at the end of the trail, her legs being shorter than Peter's, but she crested it with a little help—he finally just yanked her up as she floundered in the soft, shifting sand. They both skied down the other side, where the topography and botany of the point changed entirely. Now there was low chaparral and a hundred sand paths and dunes. Año Nuevo Island, with its ruined lighthouse, was now clearly visible.

"Where are the seals?" Peter asked. A tremendous noise similar to a motorcycle at full throttle arose. It ended with the sound of a gargantuan clogged drain.

"My God, what was that?" Peter asked, looking around in alarm.

"That was an elephant seal," Maggie said, grinning.

"Is he going to attack?" Peter asked.

"I doubt it," Maggie told him. "But if he did, we'd have about a week to get away. They don't move very fast on land."

"Where is he?"

"Probably at the end of the point on the beach. That's where the males gather this time of year to molt."

This time Maggie held out her hand, and with the background noise of several elephant seals thundering they made their way to the top of the last sand dune. This was what she had been waiting for—his reaction to his first elephant seal.

Peter stood on the sand dune and laughed for a good five minutes. "They're incredible," he said when he finally got his breath. "They were made by a committee."

A full-grown male elephant seal consists of nearly four tons of blubber encased in a scruffy grayish skin.

Attached to this gigantic sausage at the appropriate points are flippers, and attached to the head, above a thick neck, is something vaguely resembling an elephant's trunk. This gives the poor creature its name, and makes it, with all its other attributes, one of the homeliest creatures on earth. Ugly but endearing, Maggie thought.

Lying at Peter's and Maggie's feet, in a large depression in the sand, were at least a hundred seals, tightly packed together and asleep. Some were snoring, which was only natural with a nose like that. Others would open their tiny eyes, decide the sun was too hot on their delicate new skin and flip sand over themselves. And over anyone else who happened to be around. Occasionally, for no discernible reason, one of the bigger males would rear up on his front flippers, open his mouth, exposing two walruslike tusks, and let go with that incredible roar. That could set off one of two reactions: either another big one across the pack would give an answering "oh, yeah" roar or the smaller ones around the roarer would scatter as best they could, surrounded as they were by tons of blubber in bags.

Peter and Maggie stood there watching this sea of snoring, twitching, gurgling, sand-throwing, roaring creatures until an errant flipper sent a sandstorm their way. Then they moved gingerly around the edges of the herd to a dune that was not only upwind but sheltered by some bushes. From there they could see the sleeping elephant seals as well as some who seemed to be playing in the water.

Peter sat down and picked up his binoculars. "There are hundreds more out on that island. One of them is coming out the door of that abandoned house over there. Here."

He handed the binoculars to Maggie, who watched the slow, awkward progress of an elephant seal trying to get through a door. But then, she thought, their progress anywhere on lands was painfully awkward, painfully slow and, like everything else about them, extremely funny.

"Are these all males?" Peter asked. "Where are the females? Where are the babies?"

"These are all males, and they really are here getting a new coat of what passes for fur. The females were here a few months ago, had their babies and, after the babies got big enough, took them out to sea. The males will go out to sea in a month or two, and then they'll all come back for mating season next year. This is a rookery."

"Where do they go when they aren't here?"

"Nobody knows. They're just out there in the ocean somewhere. They don't come on land, except to come here."

Out of the wind and sitting side by side on the dune under the overhanging brush, they found they had to take off their parkas. Maggie rolled hers ups to make a pillow, and by wiggling managed to position herself so that she was not only semirecumbent but able to see the elephant seals in one direction and Peter in the other. She had discovered that she liked very much just looking at him. She decided to make it one of her hobbies.

He, in turn, was totally engrossed in the seals. Two of them, both old and very experienced, as could be seen from the number of scars on their thick, wrinkled necks, were sparring in the surf near the rocky beach. Rearing back on their flippers, heads back, pink mouths wide open to show their tusks, they roared and gurgled at each other until it seemed the ground would shake. Then one would collapse into the water and back off a flipper's length, while the other would trumpet his triumph. But not for long. A moment later the vanquished would rise from the water and begin to bellow again, and the victor would retreat.

"Men!" said Maggie in an I-told-you-so tone.

Peter turned to look at her with those tawny eyes. "What do you mean 'men!'?"

"They're all alike. They can't even take a bath without being macho. There aren't even any women around to see them, but they still have to make fools of themselves. And meanwhile, the females are out in fifty-degree water, taking care of the kids." Maggie, who had started that diatribe as a joke, discovered she really felt indignant about it. "They remind me of two old pols running for office."

Peter grinned. "You're right, they do. And I suppose macho men are pretty silly—Rambo is at least as ridiculous as those seals out there."

"Stop agreeing with me. That's no fun," Maggie said.

"You know what they remind me of? A bunch of yuppies at a health club."

She started to laugh, but he cut it short. "Look, I think that fellow down there has a crush on you."

At the bottom of the sand dune lay a young, medium-sized elephant seal, and he was definitely looking at Maggie. His head was on the sand, as was his proboscis, and he appeared to be breathing heavily and sighing. With each sigh, he blew up a minor sandstorm.

"I think he's very handsome. You should be flattered," Peter said.

"Maybe he's looking at you," Maggie said. "Would you be flattered?"

"That would depend on what he had in mind," said Peter. "I'd take him on at tennis, anytime. But I do believe it's you he's looking at. Maybe it's your red hair."

"Or all the rest of the things that make me a natural beauty," Maggie said, striking a cover-girl pose. "Like sand in my teeth and in my ears."

The elephant seal below them gave an especially strong snort.

"Let's try an experiment," Peter said. "Let's see how he reacts."

"Reacts to what?" Maggie asked, puzzled.

"Something like this." Peter rolled over until he was lying on his stomach beside her, and before Maggie knew it his arms were around her and his mouth had come down on hers. Maggie tensed in surprise and then gave herself up to the slow waves of warmth that began washing over her. At first his mouth was tentative, as if it really were experimental, then less so, as the kiss became deeper and deeper. His arms tightened around her, and hers around him. Her hand crept up to touch his hairline, and then his thick hair, and then to hold him closer so that the kiss would never stop. Maggie felt herself melting into him, dazed, disappearing, vanishing as a separate entity. He pulled away, and Maggie groaned, but it was only long enough to give her a tender, blazing look that spoke volumes and to kiss her eyelids, and then his mouth sought hers again.

A sound like twenty Hell's Angels revving up their bikes came from the bottom of the dune.

They both sat up instantly. The lovestruck elephant seal was humping his four thousand pounds of blubber up the sand dune at an amazing speed. There was murder in his dime-size red eyes, and it was clearly directed at Peter.

Peter and Maggie got up and ran, doubled up with laughter, until Maggie tripped and fell in the soft sand. Then she lay on her back and laughed at the sky. When she finally was able to stop, she told Peter, "You should have stayed and fought him. Rambo would have."

"I didn't have my tennis racket," said Peter. "Not only that, I don't have my parka, either. Or my binoculars."

"I left my parka back there, too." Maggie sat up. "We'll have to go back and get them."

But when they returned to the sand dune, there was a two-ton elephant seal snoring happily, exactly where they had been sitting. And no sign of the binoculars or parkas, except for a corner of blue nylon sticking out from under a flipper.

"Oh, well," Maggie said. "I never liked that parka much anyway.

The Moss Beach Distillery had once been exactly that. During Prohibition, bootleggers had made many a gallon of illegal gin there, and it had been used as a landing place and warehouse for whiskey of a better quality smuggled in from Canada. It stood on a cliff high above a secluded cove, several miles of narrow road away from the highway. Prohibition had brought prosperity to this entire coast, but with its end, the distillery and the other places like it had declined or disappeared. For fifty years the distillery had crumbled away, and then an entrepreneur had renovated it into a restaurant with a superb view of the Pacific Ocean. Most people who went there did not know of its lurid past and thought that "distillery" was just another cute name.

A starved Peter and Maggie had stopped there for dinner. For after being chased away by the elephant seal they had explored the rest of the point and done some serious beachcombing. Maggie had had wonderful luck, finding three perfect sand dollars on the leeward side of the point. Peter had found a whole stratum of fossil seashells in the cliffside but had been warned away by Maggie. "Like the elephant seals and the California poppy, they're protected by law."

Then they had started back toward San Francisco, but at a snail's pace, as it turned out. There was too much to see: classic lighthouses, a string of small, chilly beaches, fields of artichokes and brussels sprouts on low cliffs overhanging the ocean. There was the little town of Half Moon Bay, famous for its cut flowers and its fall pumpkin festival, with the eerie Navy satellite-tracking equipment beyond it. And then, off the road to the left, on the ocean, a string of small settlements, all with at least one first-class restaurant, each better than the last. Maggie had chosen the Moss Beach Distillery for its history, as well as its oysters and clams.

Peter ordered the oysters and Maggie the clams, with the agreement that they'd trade half and half. Being early, they'd gotten a window table and could look out at the dark, tree-encircled cove and the rolling breakers of the silver ocean beyond. The sun was still far above the horizon.

They chose a dry white wine from the wine list together after Maggie complained, "Just because I'm a native doesn't mean I know anything about wine." And when the food arrived they didn't talk for a while, because they were both too hungry to think of anything but eating. Maggie was starting to fill herself up on sourdough French bread and sweet butter when she realized that that was just the appetizer. She was considering ordering more oysters for the main course when Peter interrupted her thoughts.

"What's your goal in life?"

Maggie nearly choked on her wine. "Good Lord. Do you really want me to deal with that and elephant seals in one day?"

"I'm serious. Seems like something to think about after a day like this. That ocean out there, that some ancestor of ours crawled out of a million years ago, those hundred-million-year-old fossils back at Año

Nuevo, this coast right on the San Andreas Fault, which could move any minute... It makes you realize how ephemeral we really are. Or maybe the purpose of life is this: eating oysters and drinking good wine and looking out at the ocean."

Maggie was silent for a moment, thinking. "I dunno. I guess I never thought any farther than the next election. I suppose it sounds silly, but I think my goal in life would be to work on a presidential election."

"And after that?" Peter's tawny eyes were very serious, and looking directly into hers.

"After that? I never thought." Maggie felt like a lightweight. She concentrated on her last clam.

"You don't have any personal goals? Like getting married, having kids, living in a house with a picket fence and roses in the suburbs?"

That brought Maggie's head up, and she studied his face to see what was behind that question. It was as handsome as ever, and totally expressionless. "I thought about it once, getting married and having kids, but it didn't seem like a good idea. But the house in the 'burbs you can forget. Ugh. I'm a city person."

"When you thought about it, did you have a particular person in mind?"

Maggie's temper began to rise. "What is this, twenty questions? That's none of your business."

"You're right, it's not," he said in such a contrite tone and with such an apologetic look that Maggie decided to answer.

"Yes, it was with a specific person, and his name was Jim, and he had a sailboat, too. Luckily, I found out he wasn't monogamous *before* the wedding, not after." Maggie tried very hard to keep any note of sarcasm out of her voice, and nearly succeeded.

"Is this creep still around?" Peter asked, one eyebrow raised.

Maggie was toying with the empty oyster shells embedded in cracked ice on her plate. "No. He married somebody else and moved to Kansas City. I don't think he gets much sailing in there. But since then, marriage and children and picket fences have been pretty low on my list." She really didn't want to elaborate on the subject, so she turned the question on him. "And you? What's your goal in life?"

"To put A T & T back together, I guess," he said with a grin. "I didn't realize what a rotten question that was."

"I gave you an honest answer."

"I know you did. I guess I haven't thought any farther than sailing around the world. Everything after it will be an anticlimax."

"Like a wife and kids?" Maggie tried to sneak that one in sideways.

"I had an experience similar to yours. And a wife and kids would put a real crimp in my style. Besides, I have some ironclad requirements for a wife. Few can meet my standards."

"Such as?" Maggie was frankly curious now.

"She'd have to know celestial navigation."

Maggie looked over at him. He was smiling.

"And be able to jury-rig a sail, and be able to bench-press five hundred pounds," he added.

"She will be a truly impressive woman," Maggie said, straight-faced. "She doesn't have to be able to cook?"

"Only tinned beef on a galley stove. And nobody can make that edible, anyway, so it doesn't matter. Speaking of edible, what do you want to eat next?"

They decided on Dungeness crab, the dismantling and eating of which was a major obstacle to conversation. Maggie wanted to get to the subject of that round-the-world trip, but she had to wait until the remains were taken away, dessert refused and coffee served. The sun was nearly down to the horizon, and the haze magnified it into a huge red ball that appeared to be resting on the edge of the world. The ocean seemed made of molten silver.

"When are you leaving on this fantastic trip?" she asked.

"As soon as I can. Next year, I hope. I have to get everything in order."

"How long will you be gone?" Maggie discovered that she cared very much how long he would be gone.

"Two, three, four years. However long it takes."

"Will you send me a postcard?" Maggie asked plaintively.

"You bet," he said.

"Are you going solo?" Maggie tried to be diffident.

"I hope not," he said, as if he had someone in mind.

All of a sudden Maggie was sure she knew who was going on that cruise. "Who is Maria? The one your boat is named after."

"I can't tell you," he said, and then she was sure.

Maggie dropped that subject like a hot potato.

Afterward she gave herself a little lecture. He had left her at her apartment, given her a chaste little kiss in the shadows and then driven away. She had made a mad dash into the shower to get the sand out of everywhere, and then sat in her bathrobe with a towel around her head and watched, or pretended to watch, the late-night news. But even Ted Koppel, whom she professed to adore, couldn't keep her thoughts from what she had learned, or thought she had learned, today.

There was no doubt in her own mind that she was on the verge of a dangerous infatuation. It was not just his good looks.

There was little doubt that he was definitely interested in her, too. That single kiss out on the sand dune was more than enough evidence, by itself.

But exactly where that interest would lead was another matter. In that conversation about goals, which he had obviously brought up for a reason, they had both seemed to say that they weren't interested in marriage or anything beyond their near and divergent futures. Maggie had not been telling the whole truth. He seemingly had.

Where, therefore, was this leading? Answer: nowhere. In a few months he was leaving for the ends of the earth, and he was probably taking somebody named Maria with him. A relationship with him was a dead end. Anyway, even if he did ask Maggie to go along, she couldn't. She couldn't take the time off. Well, actually she could; it was a seasonal business, and between campaigns she was practically on the unemployment rolls. But that wasn't the point. Some friends of hers had sailed to Tahiti on a little boat, and they'd told her what it was like: boring and dangerous by turns. They'd been married twenty years and had gotten in their only serious quarrels out there alone in a small boat, with nobody else to talk to. Hard work and discomfort and bad food. But they'd also said that it was the most fun they'd ever had in their lives and that they'd do it again tomorrow. Maggie sighed. She'd been envious of them ever since. And, she reckoned, she had the chance of a snowball in hell of being asked to go along with Peter. He wouldn't want somebody who raised the jib upside down the first time out, who wasn't quite sure what celestial navigation was and who wouldn't spend years on a boat the size of *Maria* with an unrelated eligible bachelor. Maggie had to face facts. She was too puritanical for anything short of a marriage license along with her sailing papers.

Forget it, Maggie. Forget the whole thing now.

Maggie went to bed, her mind made up.

The first thing Maggie did when she reached the office on Monday was to call the community college about a course in celestial navigation.

Peter thought about a relationship with Maggie for a long time, too. He said the same things to himself over and over. It was hopeless. She wouldn't want to go with him to the ends of the earth. And he wouldn't, couldn't, give up a lifelong dream. Better to break it off now, when the pain would be quick and easy—like tearing off a Band-Aid—than later, when the adhesive had become part of your skin.

And then, damning himself for a fool, he called Maggie and asked if she wanted to go sailing. He was relieved and a little disappointed when she accepted. Maybe she didn't see the disaster heading their way. Or, then again, maybe she did, and didn't care.

Chapter Six

Maggie's first real clash with Fred Oliver happened on Tuesday, and it left her with ominous forebodings about how the campaign was going to go. She and Fred and Portnoy had a breakfast meeting at the City Lounge, which, like all hangouts for city hall politicians, was seedy and scruffy and had no windows. But it had great coffee and doughnuts in the morning and a happy hour every afternoon. Maggie could barely distinguish Fred's round face and bald head in the gloom. He was five feet away from her across the round table.

"Do you know," said Fred, "just who Sutter has hired as his campaign consultants?"

"No," said Portnoy. "Who?"

"He's hired Dean and Utzinger." Fred told him. "They're gunslingers."

"I never heard of 'em," said Portnoy.

"They're from Los Angeles," Maggie said. "And they're very successful down there. I don't think they've done any campaigns up here, though."

"Then it's no problem, I take it," Portnoy rumbled.

"Oh, but it is," said Fred. "They run a certain type of campaign, and we have to counter it."

"What type of campaign?"

"Negative," said Maggie. "In other words, dirty."

"I hope, Charles, that you have led a very clean life. Everything you've ever done is going to get hung out to dry," Fred Oliver said.

Portnoy did not look particularly alarmed. "Well, I've been happily married to the same woman for twenty years, I've got a big mortgage and a little house and no Swiss bank accounts," he said. "I've never plagiarized and never blown the whistle on anyone who did. What can they do to me?"

"You'd be surprised, I'm afraid," said Fred. "In fact, look forward to it."

"What can we do about it?" Portnoy asked.

"The best thing is to ignore it," Maggie replied.

"Let me put it this way," Fred told him. "There are three options. One, ignore it. Two, deny it. Three, return the fire. If you ignore it, you may be very noble, but you may be a very noble loser. If you deny it, you are spending all your time on the defensive. If you do it back, an eye for an eye, you may be able to put him on the defensive. Furthermore, it's the most cost-effective kind of campaign."

"The best thing to do is ignore it," Maggie said again.

"How do you suggest we get dirt on Sutter?" Portnoy asked.

"The same way they'll get dirt on you," Fred said. "Go through your life with a fine-tooth comb. Your public and private life, that is. Be prepared to have your garbage gone through."

"That kind of campaign always backfires," Maggie said.

"Not in L.A.," Fred argued. "And what do you know about it, anyway? You're new in the business. And you're a typical female. Be nice. Be polite. Well, that won't work. This is the big time."

Maggie was tempted to toss the dregs of her coffee at his shiny round face, but refrained. She refrained only because to have thrown it would have been following *his* campaign strategy. She opened her mouth to say something cutting, but Portnoy intervened.

"Fred, I'll have none of that around here. Save your bile for the opposition." He turned to Maggie. "You say ignore it because it will backfire. Do you have any statistics on that?"

Maggie had to admit she hadn't, but she had a gut feeling about it. She felt that San Francisco was too sophisticated a place for that kind of thing. "But it's more than that. It's one of my basic principles. Personally and politically."

Fred laughed. "There are no principles in this business."

"But I can still stick to mine," Maggie said.

"Good for you, Maggie," said Portnoy. "Anyway, I have made a decision. One of my statesmanlike ones. I have decided not to decide. In the meantime, since we have no way of knowing what they will do, we go on with the campaign as planned. We take the high road, for now, but the options are always open."

"Just remember," Fred Oliver said, "the purpose of running for office is to win, not to stick to principles."

"Maybe it's possible to do both," Maggie snapped.

The conversation at the meeting bothered Maggie for the rest of the week. It occurred to her that perhaps she was being naive. It occurred to her that maybe the end did justify the means. It also occurred to her that maybe Fred Oliver had a point: maybe she wasn't tough enough to play with the big boys.

On Sunday, sailing day, Peter called and said that though it was a beautiful day, small-craft warnings were out. High winds. So sailing was out, but he had thought of a place to go that was "safe"; did she want to go along?

"What do you mean, 'safe'?" she asked dubiously. Now that she knew what kind of campaign Sutter would be running, it was even more important that she and Peter not be seen together.

"I mean that no San Franciscan ever goes there. No one can possibly see us."

"Where is this place?" Maggie asked. "Is it very far?"

"No, quite close."

"Tell me!" she insisted.

"Just trust me. I'll give you a hint. Do you remember Edgar Allan Poe's story, *The Purloined Letter*?"

"Yes," Maggie said. "They were looking all over and it was leaning on the mantel in plain sight."

"Well, this is the same principle. I'll pick you up in an hour."

"What do I wear?"

"Jeans."

"You sure no San Franciscans ever go here?"

"Positive. I took a poll in the office."

When Peter pulled into one of the parking lots at Fisherman's Wharf, Maggie began to laugh.

"No San Franciscan ever goes here, hmm?" she said.

"Well, when was the last time you were here?"

Maggie thought. "When I was in high school, probably."

"See?"

Maggie looked at the crowds of people everywhere. "Some of these have to be San Franciscans!"

"In shorts and polyester in this climate? Carrying cameras?"

"You do have a point," she said, getting out of the car.

"I feel sick," Maggie said five hours later as she sat down on a hatch on the deck of a two-masted boat that had once brought salt cod from Alaska. They were at the Maritime Museum on the Hyde Street Pier looking at the old ships. They'd taken advantage of everything Fisherman's Wharf had to offer—from being in a fake earthquake to eating a huge double chocolate ice-cream concoction at the Chocolate Factory.

"It was the Gold Mountain High," Peter said, referring to the ice cream.

"I think it was the cotton candy," said Maggie. "Or maybe it was the clam chowder. How do the tourists do this? They must be in incredible shape. I've changed my mind. They have my total respect."

The wind gusted so hard that Maggie was nearly blown off the hatch.

"Let's go below decks," suggested Peter, "out of the wind."

Below it was dim, with shafts of sunlight coming in through the hatches. This ship was made entirely of wood, and was meant to carry cargo only, so that the deck curved with the shape of the hull. It made little groaning sounds. The Parks Service, to which the pier and the boats belonged, had put up pictures from the heyday of these cargo ships. Though the hold smelled only of sea and wood, Maggie thought she could smell salt cod. Though the pier was crowded, there was no one else down here.

They looked at the crew quarters, which made Maggie cringe. Eighteen crewmen had lived and slept in a room the size of her kitchen.

"*Maria* looks like pure luxury compared to this," Maggie said. "I wouldn't have wanted to be a sailor a hundred years ago."

"On top of that—" Peter nodded toward the room "—they had things like the lash and keelhauling."

"Why?" asked Maggie. "Why did they have to be so tough?"

"They were afraid of mutiny. A ship is like its own little kingdom when it's at sea. You can't call for help, and the sea is a very unforgiving place, a very dangerous place. You can't let your men get out of control."

"Is it still like that?"

"No, the seamen's union put a stop to it. And a book called *Two Years Before the Mast*. But they're still pretty tough on mutineers, I imagine."

"What do they do to mutineers now?" Maggie asked.

"I don't know," Peter said. "Why?"

"I was just thinking, if I go sailing with you and I get out of control, do I get keelhauled?"

"Naw," Peter said, "the punishment has to fit the crime. Probably thirty lashes and ten days in the brig, or—"

"Or what?" said Maggie.

"How's your stomach?"

"Okay. Why?" Maggie asked.

"Because," said Peter, reaching for her and pulling her close.

Maggie started to say something and then stopped. Peter was looking at her with such intensity that the words died on her lips. Then he dropped his mouth to hers. Maggie found herself involuntarily arching into him, wanting to feel the whole lean length of him, drawn like filings to a magnet. She wrapped her arms around his neck and closed her eyes and let herself go. She could feel the slow fire starting near her heart and running out through her veins, could feel her knees turning to jelly. To her distinct disappointment, Peter lifted his head and grinned down at her.

"You're sticky. Cotton candy," he said, but it didn't seem to bother him, because in a moment his mouth was on hers again, seeking, searching, demanding.

Then there were footsteps shuffling down the ladder to the hold. Peter let go and stepped back. Maggie shook herself and rearranged her features into an expression of, she hoped, polite interest. The cargo hold groaned. Or maybe it was Maggie. She couldn't tell.

Maggie watched with fascination as a pair of brown oxfords with blue socks attached to white hairy legs appeared, coming down the ladder. This was followed by a pair of khaki shorts, a paunch and a Japanese camera dangling over an obviously new sweatshirt that said California and showed a surfing scene with palm trees. The last thing to appear was a good solid American face with glasses under a baseball cap that said St. Louis Cardinals.

This apparition stopped at the bottom of the ladder, looked around, nodded at Maggie and Peter and then yelled, "Don't bother to come down, Helen, there's nothing here." Then he disappeared the way he had come.

"Nothing, huh?" Peter said, laughing. "Come on, let's go somewhere else."

They had been working their way westward, and now were nearly out of the tourist area. A high green hill rose in front of them.

Passing the ancient Italian men playing *bocce*, which consisted of throwing a heavy metal ball at other heavy metal balls, they started up the path that led around the hill. The wind was blowing fiercely, making Maggie feel that for every two steps forward she took she was forced back one step. She finally walked behind Peter, using him for a windbreak. Below them, at a dock, was yet another ship that belonged to the Maritime Museum. This one was a World War II Liberty Ship.

"What's that?" Peter asked. When Maggie explained, she was afraid for a moment that he would want to go on board that one, too. She heaved a silent sigh of relief when he said, "I've had enough ships for one day."

There were trees and a pleasant little park at the top of the hill and, rolling down from it, a long stretch of grass. There was a bench in the trees, sheltered from the wind, and they sat down on it, side by side, and looked out at the Golden Gate Bridge in the distance and the bobbing masts of the boats at the St. Francis Yacht Club.

Maggie had been horribly tempted all day long to break her own rule and ask Peter about the Sutter campaign. It was not that she was spying; it was more that she wanted to know *why* they had chosen those particular campaign consultants. But she didn't dare ask. Instead she contented herself with asking Peter, "Do you ever run into ethical problems in your work?"

"All the time," he said.

"What do you do about it? How do you decide what to do?"

"Well, it's easy for lawyers. We have a code of ethics, and we have the bar association to enforce it. Which isn't to say that all lawyers are ethical."

"That wasn't quite what I meant. I mean something more like your own personal ethics, your own principles."

"I've never run into anything yet that was against my principles that wasn't unethical, as well. Why are you asking?"

Maggie sighed. "It's just something that came up the other day. I wish my profession, if that's what it is, had a code of ethics."

"That sounds sinister," Peter said. "Also interesting. Tell me more."

"Nothing sinister. Just an argument, a discussion, that came up. Maybe I should put it this way: do you believe that the end justifies the means?"

"Do you mean as a general principle to be applied at all times?"

"I think so."

"Well, there's that old saw about all generalizations being wrong, including this one."

"That's funny, but not very helpful."

"Okay. Let me see. I believe that most of the time the end does not justify the means, but that there are exceptions, and it depends on the end, and on the means."

"That was a very lawyerly answer," Maggie said. "I'm serious. I really want your opinion."

"I don't know, Maggie." Peter said. "I'd have to know all the circumstances. I think it's a relative thing—how good or bad the end is, and how good or bad the means. It's that old argument about 'What if you had been given the chance to assassinate Hitler in 1936?' Murder is wrong, but Hitler was worse."

"And there I am back to go again," said Maggie. "At least I don't have to assassinate anyone." Except for character assassination, she added to herself. "I think I'll stick to my principles. At least I'll have a clear conscience."

"That's one of the nicer things to have," Peter said. "Can you tell me what that's all about? Or is it a campaign secret?"

"No and yes." Maggie grinned. "I shouldn't have even brought it up. You evaded it, anyway."

"Never ask a lawyer for a straight answer," said Peter. "But I'm always good for a crooked one."

"At two hundred dollars an hour, too, I'll bet."

"Close. Next to robbing banks, it's the most lucrative profession in the world. And in America we have it down to a fine art You can't sneeze without hiring one of us."

"Didn't Shakespeare say something about lawyers?" Maggie said.

"Yeah, he has a character say, 'First thing we do, let's kill all the lawyers.'"

"Well, Shakespeare didn't say a word about campaign consultants, I'll bet," Maggie said happily.

"Sure he did," said Peter.

"What?"

"Out, damned spot." He grinned. "And in both cases the end justifies the means."

"Maybe I *should* be more like Lady Macbeth," Maggie said, pensively. "Go for the jugular. Shoot from the hip."

"I thought you were into campaigns, not blood-baths," Peter said. "Maybe I should tell Bill Sutter to hire a bodyguard."

Thirty ripostes to that ran through Maggie's mind, but she said none of them.

After a while they wandered back through the still-energetic crowds to the car, where there was an argument about what restaurant no San Franciscans ever went to. They settled on an Italian place on tacky gaudy Broadway, next to a topless joint. The pasta was plastic and the sourdough stale and Maggie thought longingly of the great Italian restaurants only a few blocks away, over the hill in North Beach. She wasn't very hungry, luckily.

They had to walk the length of Broadway to get to and from the car, and each way were accosted by barkers telling them of the supposed delights inside each of the shoddy nightclubs.

In the car, Peter said, "Well, how does it feel to be a tourist in your own hometown?"

"I had a great time at Fisherman's Wharf. That was fun. But Broadway—yuk."

"When the campaign is over and we can be seen together, we won't have to go to places like that. I'll take you to all the best places and show you off."

"Don't get your hopes up," said Maggie gloomily. "I don't think this campaign is ever going to be over. It's just started, and it already feels like a year."

"Do you want to go somewhere else? Have a nightcap?"

"No, thanks," Maggie said, touching the top of her head. "I think I want to go home and get the cotton candy out of my hair. I have a big week coming up. All of them seem to be big weeks now.''

Peter double-parked and walked her to her door, and they stood and talked, holding hands and kissing occasionally in the shadows by the door until a car began honking in the street.

"Okay, okay," Peter muttered, turning toward his car. "Sailing next weekend for sure," he told Maggie. "Small-craft warnings or not."

"It's Opening Day, anyway," Maggie said. "The weather wouldn't dare be bad."

"What's Opening Day?"

"You'll see," said Maggie.

There was an angry blast from the street.

Peter ran for his car, and Maggie unlocked the door and went inside. She skipped up the two flights of stairs, and when she got into her apartment she headed straight for the shower, where she stayed until the hot water ran out, clear through five complete renditions of "Memories" sung off-key at the top of her lungs.

Chapter Seven

Maggie worked late every night that week, some-times until nearly midnight, but she was determined to have a free day on Sunday, if not for Peter, then for The Event. It was Opening Day, the official unoffi-cial beginning of the sailing season on San Francisco Bay, a body of water upon which there was year-round sailing. Opening Day was purely arbitrary.

By the time they got to the Sausalito dock, there was a perfect blue sky, and a perfect breeze. Opening Day was a day when you didn't do much sailing, even though you'd be out on your boat most of the time. So a light breeze was enough.

There were a thousand boats on the water when they crossed the bridge, and another thousand by the time they got sleek little *Maria* out of Richardson Bay and into San Francisco Bay itself.

Peter was following instructions from Maggie. It was his first Opening Day, though he probably had, Maggie guessed, a pretty good idea of what was going to happen. With so light a breeze and so clear a sky, it was gloriously warm, and both Maggie and Peter were dressed in shorts and T-shirts, though she had already warned him to bring a change of clothes.

"We need to go around Angel Island and get in line," Maggie told him. "The destroyer is anchored in Raccoon Strait, between Belvedere and Angel Island."

"The destroyer? As in Navy vessel? I thought this was an occasion to bless the boats in the Bay."

"It is," Maggie said. "The Navy uses a destroyer for a platform for the priest. And the rabbi, and the minister. This is an ecumenical blessing."

They sailed slowly across the traffic-jammed bay, rounded Angel Island and found themselves in the midst of wall-to-wall boats. There were sloops and ketches and yawls and rowboats and sport fishing boats and Boston whalers and the Coast Guard and stinkpots and converted tugboats and even a few windsurfers and kayaks and a raft or two, and something that looked suspiciously like a bathtub.

Peter looked on, amazed and amused. Looming over them all, far ahead, was indeed a good gray Navy destroyer.

And though it was only ten-thirty in the morning, the party had already started. Music was coming from various boats, people were shouting back and forth at their friends, and a windsurfer catching an errant breeze managed to somehow wend his way through this conglomeration stark naked—a streaker. There were cheers, and the sound of champagne corks popping. Overhead, a huge white blimp puttered back and forth.

Maggie had brought a bottle of champagne, but she didn't want to open it yet.

"It's going to be a while before we get our turn at being blessed," Peter said. "What do we do in the meantime?"

"I think lying in the sun would be just fine," Maggie said, stripping down to her bathing suit. "I can take at least five minutes of this sun."

She stretched out on her stomach on one of the long benches under the coaming and peered through her sunglasses at Peter, who was leaning against the cockpit, watching her every move with an appreciative eye.

Maggie had been waiting since Wednesday for this moment and had devoted considerable time to deciding where and how to ask the questions she wanted to ask. It seemed to her that Peter was being deliberately reserved, and that there was a whole lot she didn't know about him.

"What do you really do for a living?" she asked innocently.

"What do you mean? I'm an attorney."

"I know that. But you said you did really boring stuff."

"I think I said it was boring to everyone but me," he said, one dark eyebrow raised.

"The *Chronicle* doesn't think it's boring. There was an article in there last week, with your name in it," Maggie said, very casually.

Peter looked surprised. "There was? What was it about?"

"The Rincon Oil takeover."

"Oh, that. What did it say about me?"

"It quoted you as saying something about 'All's fair in love and war.'"

"Yeah, I remember that. Do you generally read the business pages?"

"I read the whole paper, front to back," Maggie confessed. "But I have a little trouble on the business pages. There is a whole different vocabulary: poison pills, golden parachutes, greenmail, shark repellent. I take it you are working for Leon Dickens, the famous corporate raider. He swallows up innocent little corporations before they know what's happened to them."

"Leon Dickens may be a villain in the press, but his takeover raids aren't always bad. Sometimes the innocent little corporation isn't so innocent. Sometimes it's a great big one, like Rincon, and sometimes it's so badly managed that the stockholders and the employees and even the economy are suffering. I think Leon Dickens, and the other raiders sometimes—" and here he looked Maggie straight in the eye "—sometimes do a lot of good. But not always."

Maggie sat up and faced him. "But you wouldn't work for someone like that if you didn't think it was a good cause."

It wasn't a question, but he treated it as one. "Good and bad don't enter into it. I'm really just one of the bunch of lawyers working on this acquisition, and my real concern, like everyone else's, is that it be legal. That it conform to the rules.''

Maggie was appalled. "That quote, 'All's Fair in Love and War.' What did you mean by that?''

"I think I was referring to something Rincon did, as a matter of fact, not something Dickens did.''

"So Rincon did something bad, and you excused it with that?'' Maggie was already turning red from the sun, so she moved until she was in the shade of the sail. That happened to be where Peter was.

He put his arms around her. "Maggie, look around here. This is not the place to be discussing this. But I want to say something, and I want you to listen closely. Rincon did something that corporations do to stave off takeover bids. It was good or bad only in that it saved or did not save the company, and only if you think the company needs saving. Lawyers don't, can't, make moral judgments. They follow the law. It can be a good law or a bad law, but it's still to be followed until changed. Criminal lawyers have to defend murderers and rapists and have to give them the best possible defense, even when they know they are guilty. It's following the rules of our system of justice, the best one in the world. If we started making moral judgments, we wouldn't have a system of laws anymore, we'd have a system of individual human beings making individual moral judgments. That's going back four thousand years. The law is all that stands between civilization and savagery.''

It was a long lecture, and Maggie had some trouble concentrating on it. Peter's proximity, his arms around her, the music, the laughter around them, had all combined to make her original point flee from her brain. She leaned against him and said, "I understand." She probably did, she thought, but she no longer cared.

"Good," he said. "Now I think it's our turn to get blessed."

One by one the bathtubs, sloops, whalers and ketches were sailing or chugging past the destroyer. Peter maneuvered *Maria* into line, and they slowly, under both sail and motor, approached the destroyer. Peter looked ahead and saw an occasional round, shiny object in the air. From ahead of them came whoops of laughter.

"They're throwing something at the people on the deck of the destroyer," he said, puzzled.

"Is the destroyer throwing anything back?" Maggie asked.

"I can't tell," he told her.

Maggie grinned. "Well, batten down the hatches and prepare for attack. Newport has the America's Cup, but San Francisco has Opening Day." She ducked into the cockpit and came out wearing a rain jacket.

"What's that for?" Peter asked suspiciously.

"You'll see."

The first water balloon, clearly aimed at someone else, landed on the deck and exploded harmlessly at Peter's feet. The second bounced off the mast and exploded all over both Peter and Maggie. The third one, which came in low and slow, Peter caught.

"Now I'm armed," he said, grinning from ear to ear. "Why didn't you tell me to bring some of these?"

"Because I didn't want to spoil the surprise." Maggie smiled. The real reason had been that she hadn't known how he would take it. Sometimes he seemed so, well, serious, especially about sailing. So eastern. He was still an alien to her.

"Incoming at twelve o'clock," yelled Peter, and she saw a bright blue balloon coming at her out of the sun. She reached out for it, but it slid through her hands and hit her on the shoulder, knocking her back against the coaming and thoroughly drenching her. She lay there laughing helplessly and hearing laughter from the boat from which the balloon had come.

They had three more intact balloons by the time they reached the destroyer. High above them on the navy ship's deck stood three clergymen, all of them soaking wet. Beside the three was a wooden contraption manned by a sailor with a huge grin on his face.

"What's that?" asked Maggie, but before the words were out of her mouth, she knew.

The ketch ahead of them had lobbed a balloon at the destroyer. The men of the cloth ducked nicely, and one of them signaled the sailor. From the wooden contraption came a water balloon flying at approximately the speed of sound, accurately aimed dead center on the deck of the ketch. Water flew everywhere, and the boat rocked.

"It's a catapult," Peter said unnecessarily. "It's our turn. Prepare to take cover." He overhanded one of the captured enemy balloons neatly at the feet of the priest.

Maggie ducked into the cockpit and only heard the thump and the shower of the retaliatory strike.

"I think it's more of a baptism that a blessing," Peter advised her.

When she came back out, they were away from the destroyer and beside a giant fifty-footer, from the deck of which came much merriment and noise. Maggie couldn't resist. Taking a nice fat red balloon, she threw it at the source of the noise with all her strength. There was a collective yell, and a veritable barrage of balloons inundated *Maria*.

Peter, soaked from head to foot, dripping, changed courses, trimmed the sail and said, "That's demented. And that includes the Navy and the clergy."

"You ain't seen nothin' yet," Maggie told him.

The long parade of boats made a huge loop across the bay, gliding past the docks of the city, showing off their decorations, of which there were many, and occasionally lobbing a water balloon at an unsuspecting crowd onshore, if they could get close enough. The only disaster so far was the bathtub, which began to ship too much water and had to be rescued by the Coast Guard. As many boats as possible headed for anchorages at Hospital Cove at Angel Island.

Peter and Maggie changed into dry clothes, hauled out the cooler and ate lunch, chatting with people in boats on all sides. Bottles of wine were passed back and forth, along with hors d'oeuvres, beers and jokes. Some people climbed from boat to boat, spreading cheer. It was, Peter remarked, like a huge floating picnic. Peter popped the champagne cork, setting off a barrage from other boats, all of them aimed at a little green sloop anchored nearby. Maggie remembered seeing it before on the Bay. It had a spinnaker with a cartoon frog on it, and its name was *Ribit*.

Lazing in the sun with the champagne, Peter said, "What next?"

"You'll see," Maggie said smugly, though she wasn't sure herself. Every year was different.

Just as she finished speaking, strains of band music floated across the water, and around the headland next to Raccoon Strait chugged an old ferryboat. Maggie could see a phalanx of tubas on the top deck. "Oh, when the saints, go marching in..." roared the band, and a tremendous cheer arose from the boats. The ferryboat stopped outside Hospital Cove, and a huge red-and-white banner was unfurled down its side: Stanford Marching Band.

Cheers and boos.

"The boos are from the University of California people," Maggie explained. "Stanford and U.C. are like Harvard and Yale. They hate each other."

"I already knew that." Peter had to yell to be heard over the Stanford fight song.

Then, to Maggie's astonishment, and to gasps that could be heard from the other boats, the band blazed into the beginnings of the fight song of the archenemy University of California. The tuba players moved to the back rail of the ferry, which now faced the cove, and in perfect unison elaborately turned their backs and dropped their pants.

There was an explosion of cheers, catcalls, yells, applause and laughter.

"They did worse at one of the football games and got banished for months," Maggie said. "They're really raunchy."

Peter laughed. "I've seen worse. Columbia is the Stanford of the Ivy League."

The band, which played a lot better than it behaved, Maggie commented, ran through a couple more songs, without incident and to much applause. The ferry started up again and headed toward Sausalito, as the band tootled a derisive "Sailing, Sailing, over the Bounding Main."

"The thing to do now," Maggie said, "is follow it, to see where they're going. That's where the best party will be."

"At least the loudest," Peter countered. "We might as well stow this stuff and go."

There were parties going on at every yacht club around the Bay. But the loudest one was at the Sausalito Yacht Club, and to get to it they had to anchor far out, inflate the dinghy and row in. To Peter's surprise, they were not turned away at the dock.

"I don't even *know* anybody who belongs here," he said.

"I don't, either, but they don't care. At least not today," Maggie said.

Inside the ramshackle clubhouse, decorated with the burgees of a hundred other yacht clubs and some paintings of ships under sail, a much smaller Stanford band was playing ear-splitting rock music. The rest of the band, identifiable by their mismatched uniforms, were lolling around, drinking beer and dancing. Maggie lost Peter within two minutes, and within another two had danced with the president of the club and with his fifteen-year-old grandson. The grandfather was the better dancer, Maggie thought. Better sense of rhythm. She had shouted at him that she was a party-crasher, and he had shouted back that he had the power to make her an honorary member.

After four or five more partners, she caught sight of Peter gyrating in the middle of the floor with a voluptuous blonde who clearly wanted more of him than a minute on the dance floor. Maggie watched for a few moments, excused herself and threaded her way through the dancers. It was a dangerous activity. Her foot got stomped once, and she barely avoided an elbow in her eye. Just as she reached Peter, the music stopped abruptly, as did the wild motion on the floor. She linked an arm through his and said, "Oh, I've been looking all over for you" as possessively as possible. She was happy to see a look of chagrin on the blonde's face.

Peter looked down at her with curiosity. "You weren't jealous or anything, were you?"

"Who, me? Jealous? Don't be ridiculous," Maggie said.

"I got a couple of drinks for us, but I couldn't find you, so I put them down somewhere over here."

He was able to find the glasses, but they were empty.

"Now what?" Peter said. "You're the expert."

"We could dance," Maggie told him.

"Only if it's slow," Peter replied. "I don't mind keeping my distance from that blonde, but you I want to get close to."

"I doubt if the Stanford band knows anything slow."

"We could request 'Sailing, Sailing over the Bounding Main.'"

Maggie tried to imagine what kind of dance could be done to that, and the idea was so ludicrous she began giggling.

Somebody fell off the dock. There was a tremendous splash and some yelling before he was pulled out with a boat hook.

The band came back and zoomed into "Stayin' Alive."

"Amazing. They know classical music," Peter shouted.

"What?" Maggie yelled.

"Never mind, it wasn't important."

"That blonde is headed over here."

"What?" Peter yelled.

"That blonde is coming looking for you." Maggie stood on tiptoe to shout in Peter's ear.

"Then let's blow this joint."

"What?" Maggie said, but it was too late. The blonde had dragged Peter, who seemed to be protesting but little, into the crowd on the dance floor, and she herself was being importuned to dance by the person who had fallen off the dock. Or so she reasoned, as he was the only dripping-wet person in the room. It was another hour before she and Peter saw each other and could talk, and that was in the dinghy.

Peter was rowing back to the boat, and Maggie was being as unhelpful as possible, sitting on the bottom of the dinghy with her arms around her legs and her chin on her knees.

"I did *not* dance with him because you were dancing with that blonde," Maggie said, "and he wasn't drunk, he just slipped off the dock."

"A likely story." Peter sneered. "You could have rescued me from that blonde, whose name happens to be Doris, any time."

"You're a big boy, you can rescue yourself. I think you wanted to dance with her."

"I think you're jealous. Is that it?"

"That's the second time today you've said that. No, I'm not jealous. I think you're jealous of the guy who fell off the dock, whose name happens to be George."

"George, huh?"

"Yeah, George."

"You seeing George again?"

"You seeing Doris again?"

"If I want to. We never signed anything in this relationship."

"You call this a relationship?" Maggie laughed.

"Correction. It's a slight acquaintance," Peter said. "We never defined anything about it."

"What's there to define? It's a dead end," Maggie flung out. "Going nowhere. No, that's wrong. I'm going nowhere, you're going to Fiji."

"That's wrong, too. You're going upward and onward. The presidential campaign, remember? We're just going two different directions, like everybody else in the world."

"The relationship is still a dead end, Peter, don't you see that?"

"Not as long as I'm not in Fiji," he said. "I don't care how it sounds, I'm jealous as hell of George the drunk. I admit it. Okay?"

"He's not a drunk, and I'm jealous of Doris with the bottle of peroxide. I admit that, too. Now what do we do?"

"Kiss and make up?" Peter said, just as they reached *Maria*.

"Beats what we've been doing," Maggie said, pulling herself over the rail.

Chapter Eight

If Maggie had had her way, the kissing-and-making-up part would have begun immediately, but Peter, as boatowner, had his way first. And his way required deflating the dinghy, weighing anchor, motoring the short way to the berth, taking down the jib and storing it, coiling the sheets, snapping the cover on the mainsail and clearing out the boat. With all deliberate speed.

Then everything had to be carried to the car, which was clearly not a good place for kissing and making up, sitting as it was in a dusty dirt parking lot surrounded by huge rolls of wire and large pieces of rusted metal that had had something to do with boats once. Peter did not berth his boat at a yacht club.

Then he drove—very slowly, Maggie thought—up Bridgeway, the main street of Sausalito, and up the winding road that meandered everywhere before it finally emptied into Highway 101, just before the Golden Gate Bridge. He crept across the bridge, although no one seemed to be passing them, and waited with the patience of a turtle in the lines in front of the tollbooths. At the tollbooth itself, he wasted precious time, carrying on a long conversation with the tolltaker:

"Sorry I haven't got anything smaller than a twenty."

"That's okay, sir. Have a good day."

After that, he took the long way, Maggie thought, until she realized she didn't know where he was going. When she finally figured it out, she still knew more shortcuts than he did, though she excused him for that, since she was a native and he wasn't. And when they finally got there, there wasn't any place to park, and Peter had to circle and circle, even though there were several places a native San Franciscan would have parked—sideways on a corner, or on the sidewalk. Maggie began to wonder if he had forgotten that they were going to kiss and make up, at a bare minimum.

Finally somebody pulled out, and Peter backed into the parking place with one swing, a neat job, and then the car had to be unloaded, and two blocks walked—uphill. Slowly. Up. The. Steps. The lock on the downstairs door took forever to get open, and the two flights of stairs took longer, and then there were the locks on the apartment door.

Peter walked into the apartment, dumped everything he was carrying on the kitchen table, signaled to Maggie to do the same, picked up Genghis Khat from his comfortable perch on the back of the couch, carried him to the spare bedroom, tossed him in and locked the door. Then he came back to where Maggie was standing in the living room, looking at the pencil line on the map of the world, gazing at names like Coral Sea, Tawi Tawi, Zamboanga, Bali and Straits of Malacca and fidgeting.

"Now," Peter said, and took her in his arms.

His mouth came down on hers, warm and cool and soft and demanding all at the same time. The tension in Maggie was gone instantly, and her limbs turned to Jell-O. But just before her knees gave way, his arm slid under them, and without taking his mouth from hers he carried her to the couch, laying her gently on it.

Maggie opened her arms to him, and before she understood how or why, he was lying on top of her, not heavily, braced on his elbows looking down at her. He looked at her with that blaze in his eyes that she'd seen before, looked as if he were going to say a world of things, but he did not. He only said, very softly, "Oh, Maggie," and began to kiss her eyes, her hairline, her nose, her chin, her neck, only to return each time to her mouth in a kind of agony.

Maggie, without volition, found herself arching against him so that her softer, rounded body could sense every inch of his square-planed, harder one. Slow, sweet fire was building from some central core inside her and beginning to trail out along her nerves and muscles, giving them a warmth and life of their own. She could not get enough of him.

His tongue began exploring the warm interior of her mouth, and her hypersensitized hands began exploring his neck, his back under the black sweater he wore, wherever they could reach. His skin was smooth-rough and warm-cold and soft-hard.

And then his hands began to follow the trail of his mouth, first on her face, and then her chin and her neck and then to the V-neck of *her* black sweater, and Maggie decided that she was on the very verge of expiring with desire. But, as with his deliberateness with his boat, he could not be hurried at this, either, and nothing Maggie could do, no signal she could give with hand or body, could increase the achingly dilatory manner in which he was bewitching her body, turning it into his own.

At long last, his hand slid under the sweater and began moving up until his fingers could trace the outline of her breasts, and Maggie arched again so that he could reach the fasteners on her bra. He pulled up bra and sweater together, looked at her for a long time and said, "You're really beautiful, you know," and after that he pulled the sweater back down and pulled Maggie to a sitting position and said, "I think it's best to stop there. I'm sorry. I don't know what came over me."

Maggie sagged, looking at him, appalled. It was as if he'd thrown a bucket of cold water over her.

But he jumped up from the couch and went over and stood by the window. Maggie saw that he was not looking at the view, but at her.

"I think you're right," he said. "I think there's no future in this. We're two people going in completely opposite directions. And if we had ended up doing what we were headed for a few minutes ago, it could have been fatal." His voice was as cold as the imaginary bucket of water.

"I don't understand," Maggie said, but she did.

"Put it this way: I'm trying very hard not to fall in love with you, and I'm afraid I already have. I can't afford that. I have to leave; you have to stay. I don't like being in love, I don't like feeling jealous, I don't like what it does to my concentration, I don't like the chaos that it makes of my life." Now his voice was glum.

"I feel the same way," Maggie said. "It's true. You're right."

"You feel the same way?"

"Yeah. But maybe I can talk myself out of it." Maggie sighed. "'Tis better to have loved and lost..."

"...than never to have loved at all," Peter finished for her.

"I guess I'd better go," Maggie said, standing up and straightening her clothes.

"Don't go yet," Peter said quickly. "Stay and have a...a cup of coffee."

"I really should go. There are things I have to do at home." Maggie started toward the door. She was feeling, she had to admit, not nearly as bad as she should. There was, in fact, a certain...nobility in what they were doing. Renouncing each other for the sake of each other. Héloïse and Abélard, Romeo and Juliet, Antony and Cleopatra. Horrible examples all. Maggie didn't want to go into a convent or take an "apothecary's draught" or have to end up holding an asp. She hated snakes. She was only a little bit noble, then. But, as with love, a little nobility was better than nothing.

"Penny for your thoughts," Peter said.

"Not even worth that," Maggie replied.

He took her home, helped her carry he stuff in and left her with a handshake at the door. She fixed herself a frozen dinner in the microwave, ate it while watching TV and was fifteen minutes into what she thought was a public television show on the ecological niche of giraffes before she realized that what she was watching was *Hot Rods to Hell*. She was concentrating on nobility when the phone rang.

She got it on the first ring, even though she spilled a lot of sauce from her plate doing it. She could tell from the ring who it was.

"Hello?"

"Hi, it's me."

"Hi."

"Just wanted to know if you were okay. Big day today."

"I'm fine."

"You sure?"

"Sure, I'm sure."

"Uh, look, Maggie, I had an idea. I've been thinking. I'm not going anywhere for months and months—I can't leave until March at least, because of the winter storms. That's a long time. We've had a good time, haven't we? I mean, don't you think we get along well, as friends? Interested in the same things and all?"

"What are you leading up to, Peter?"

"A man and a woman don't have to be lovers, do they? Can't they just be friends? See each other in the regular course of events, without making lifelong commitments?"

"Some of them can."

"Do you think we could?"

"It's a pretty dumb idea, considering what just happened, but we could try."

"I knew you'd understand. Want to go sailing next weekend? In fact, do you want to really learn how to sail? I'll teach you."

"No more upside-down jibs?"

"That's a promise."

Maggie hung up the phone. "Fool," she said to herself.

Peter hung up the phone. "Damn fool," he said to himself. The thought had crossed his mind that he would give up sailing around the world for Maggie. He suppressed it immediately.

Chapter Nine

The next morning, Maggie found a message on her answering machine when she got out of the shower. It was Fred Oliver's voice, asking her to come directly to Portnoy campaign headquarters. Something important had happened over the weekend. She could not tell from the tone of his voice whether the event was good or bad, but whatever it was, it was urgent. She was dressed and out of the apartment in ten minutes.

When she arrived at the rented former auto dealership, cavernous and echoing, she found Portnoy, Fred Oliver and two of his campaign workers huddled over a scarred table in a corner away from the huge show windows. The symbol of the political campaign, the Styrofoam cup with the dregs of bad coffee in it, was everywhere.

"What's up?" Maggie asked, concerned.

"Look at this," Fred Oliver said. "What do you make of it?"

He handed Maggie a letter. It read:

Dear Charles Portnoy:
William Sutter was suspended for a year at Yale for cheating. Here is his transcript to prove it.

                                                A Friend

"Good Lord," said Maggie. "Is there really a transcript?"

He handed her two stapled pieces of paper that looked very like a college transcript. Maggie felt it. The seal of the university was embossed on it, over the registrar's signature.

"I think it's real," Maggie decided.

"So do we," Fred Oliver agreed. "The question is, how do we use it best? What's the result of the latest polling? Thursday, wasn't it?"

"Neck and neck," Maggie said. "Sutter ahead by four points, but that's almost the degree of error."

"I think this is worth at least ten points," Oliver said. "I think a press conference."

"Do you really have to use it?" Maggie asked.

"I beg your pardon?" said Fred Oliver. "Are you serious? Is there any good reason not to use it?"

"I can give you some good ones," Maggie said. "First, it's unethical and makes me feel sleazy; two, it happened a long time ago and isn't relevant to anything; and three—and this is the real reason we shouldn't use it—it'll backfire. Sutter is running a good clean campaign, and it will just get him the sympathy vote."

Fred Oliver's face began to redden. "You are dead wrong. If the charge is true, it reflects on Sutter's character, and negative campaigns *do* work. I promise you. I know."

"Really, Fred? Name one that worked in this district. Maybe they work other places, but not in San Francisco. Call Ted up; he'll tell you how sophisticated these voters are. He knows every one of them by his first name."

"That piece of paper is the thing that will win this campaign, and that is what I am here to do," Fred nearly yelled. "I am not so sure about your motives, though. Just whose side are you on, Maggie?"

"May I cut in?" Charles Portnoy's rumbling voice drowned out Fred's last words. "After all, this is my campaign, and I think that I should have something to say about it. And I'm with Maggie. We don't use it."

"You're making a big mistake," Fred Oliver said. "They'd do it to you, if they had something on you."

"And it would backfire on them. I didn't just fall off the turnip truck into politics, my friend. We don't use it." Portnoy looked at his watch. "I have to be at a neighborhood coffee session in ten minutes."

"How many of those things have you been to?" Maggie asked.

"All of them," sighed Portnoy. "I'm like Ted. I know every voter in the Fifth District by his first name."

* * *

The San Francisco summer was upon them, full blast. Day after day, the fog was there at dawn, cleared for a minute and a half at noon and then rolled back in again during the afternoon. A hundred thousand tourists inundated the city daily and were in turn inundated by chill fog. Maggie, like other residents, only laughed a little when she saw people in shorts, T-shirts and goose bumps hanging off the cable cars.

The weather forecasters had an easy time of it these months. "Coastal fog, hot inland," they predicted every day, and they were always right. This was Peter's first summer, and he somewhat plaintively asked Maggie when the sun was going to come out. That was easy: "About the fifteenth of September, for three days." Maggie refrained from quoting him the famous Mark Twain crack—"the coldest winter I ever spent was summer in San Francisco"—knowing full well that thirty other people would be only too happy to quote it at him.

Sometimes, when they drove across the Bridge to sail *Maria*, the fog sat right on the deck of the bridge, so that the towers completely disappeared. Other times, it unrolled itself down the Marin hills, stealthily hugging the ground, sneaking in like a thief. Once in a while the whole Bay would be clear, but most often they sailed in the fog—when it wasn't too thick.

It was eerie. The neat little boat would be sailing along in bright sunshine one minute and into a cloud the next, with streamers of fog blowing by, and murky glimpses of other boats in the distance.

Maggie was learning. But there was much she didn't know, she realized, like the names of things; "cringle," "roach," "batten," "crutch."

"I thought," she said to Peter, "that sailing terms were romantic and beautiful. Those words aren't."

"How about 'bilge' and 'gudgeons'?" Peter asked. "Those are nice and romantic."

"I like 'beating to windward' and 'wing and wing' and 'close-hauled' and 'heave-ho.'"

Peter laughed. "You mean 'heave to,' don't you? I think only Volga boatmen say 'heave-ho.'"

Maggie refused to admit error. "Pirates do, too. That's what I meant."

"Of course. Now, ready about!"

And Maggie jumped for the jib sheet to pull it in to come about. At first she hadn't had the strength to pull it tight enough, but after many days of sailing she could do it like a seasoned racer. Peter had not been kidding when he'd said he would teach her to sail. He drove her mercilessly.

But sometimes she wondered what she would ever do with all her newfound knowledge and muscle. After Peter left, she would not have anyone to sail with. She did not imagine that sailing alone would be much fun. Maybe, she thought, she'd get so rich from her successful campaign business that she could buy and berth a boat like *Maria*. But that was all she would do, she thought, let it sit in a dock, and go look at it once in a while.

Their "relationship," such as it was after their mutual confessions of the necessity of not falling in love with each other, had been very friendly—period. And related to sailing, period. They were careful not to get unnecessarily close to one another for fear of sparks flying, and there were certain subjects they didn't mention, and certain words they never used. Maggie was not happy with this, nor was she particularly unhappy. When she thought about it, she stressed the nobility of it all. But usually she was too tired to think about anything much except getting her head on the pillow before she fell asleep. She was too busy to think.

And so, evidently, was Peter. Though he rarely mentioned it, the Rincon Oil acquisition had become national news—in fact, Leon Dickens, the raider, had made the cover of *Newsweek*, and as the article reported, there were those who thought him a great entrepreneur and those who thought him a shark. Rincon, *Newsweek* said, had thought of everything from poison pills to greenmail to try to squirm away, but now there was a white knight in the offing. Maggie read the article and decided to leave it at that. She knew Peter was working six days a week, and most evenings. She didn't ask.

They saw each other one night at the Sheraton Palace Hotel, where Portnoy and Sutter appeared before the prestigious Commonwealth Club after a dinner of dry veal and excellent mousse. Maggie had been acting as a kind of temporary advance man for Portnoy, and thus her dinner was free.

The Commonwealth Club was famous for grilling candidates and public officials mercilessly with sharp written questions from the audience. In spite of this, or because of this, few refused an invitation to speak in front of them, and sometimes even presidents begged for the chance. There was always television coverage, often national. It was, Maggie thought, terrific exposure for Portnoy. Both he and Sutter were doing well, though Maggie guessed that the audience would be more inclined toward Sutter at the polls. The Commonwealth Club's members were more his type. Few had ever been in law enforcement.

Sutter had fielded questions about the Middle East, the federal sewage project and saving the Bay. Portnoy had held his end up on gill-net fishing, Japanese computer chips and the newly revived Peripheral Canal. A man stood up in the audience and asked both candidates for their position on something Maggie could not quite make out, and she twisted in her seat to see who he was. Peter was leaning against the wall at the back of the room, looking straight at her. He smiled slightly and looked away.

Maggie missed what the man was saying, and missed what the roar of laughter afterward was all about.

She asked the svelte white-haired woman seated next to her what it was all about.

"He seemed to be saying that he was *for* toxic waste."

"How can anybody be *for* toxic waste? Who was he?" Maggie asked.

"I don't know," said the woman. "He's certainly not a member."

Afterward, as everyone was filing out and Maggie was making her way through the television cables toward Portnoy to congratulate him, she caught sight of Peter again. He was smiling down at a young woman in a full-length mink coat. The only thing more beautiful than that coat, Maggie thought, was the cameo face of its wearer. She felt a terrible—and unwelcome—pang. When she reached Portnoy, he said, "You look pale. Are you all right?"

Maggie, too, was spending most of her time in the office. She considered bringing in a sleeping bag but decided against it. More than once she suspected that Ted had slept there. She'd arrive in the morning and find him groggy and wrinkled, but working. She'd had three more phone lines installed, so that she could hang up on more people accidentally, and added a second computer terminal.

The Portnoy campaign invested in a major telephone survey to learn just what issues should be raised, and what shouldn't. Ted took the results and fine-tuned them, and Maggie called a meeting.

"First and foremost, the issue right now is offshore oil drilling," Maggie told an unsurprised Portnoy.

"I'm agin it, of course," he said. "I refuse to come out in favor of oil slicks on the Bay."

"So is everybody in San Francisco, and so will Sutter be." Maggie said. No problem on that. "Preservation of the coastline?"

"Only a developer could be against that," Portnoy said.

"But you'd better come up with a plan to preserve it," Maggie advised. "Something simple and effective."

"You'll have it in your hands tomorrow," Portnoy said facetiously.

"Taxes? The deficit?"

"Raise the first to cover the second," Portnoy said instantly.

"Careful," warned Fred Oliver. "That's not likely to be a popular position."

"Nationally, no, but in the Fifth District, would you believe, a majority were for increased taxes," Maggie said. "Remember, we live in a different world."

"What will Sutter do?" Oliver asked.

"He can do the same thing we did—a poll—and probably did," Maggie said. "We'll have to wait and see."

"Maggie, my advice to our client here is to waffle on that until we can do another poll. I don't trust your research. Nobody is for increased taxes. And I have been in this business a lot longer than you have. I believe my judgment is better."

Maggie could hear him mentally adding, "You little pip-squeak."

"Okay, okay, you two," Portnoy said, "we'll have a definite maybe on increased taxes. What else? This is fun."

Maggie held out a sheaf of papers. "About fifty more issues. Then we can decide which ones to push."

Portnoy groaned and put his head in his hands. "I take it back," he said.

That evening, Maggie went to her celestial navigation class. She was doing well on paper, but the skies had been so overcast all summer that no one in the course had seen a real star, much less the polestar, to navigate by. She learned that there was no fixed star equivalent to Polaris in the Southern Hemisphere and wondered how early sailors without instruments had navigated from, say, the Sunda Straits, to Mauritius. For she, too, had bought a globe and a huge world map and was making up imaginary, purely imaginary, routes around the world in the odd moments before she fell asleep at night. She would follow him in her imagination when he left.

In early September there came a lull, both in the campaign and in the fog. Peter and Maggie sailed two days in a row, with Maggie paying special attention to what she thought was the hardest part of sailing, especially on the crowded Bay: the rules of the road.

"Sail has right-of-way over power," Maggie said.

"But never argue with a supertanker," Peter reminded her.

"A sailboat close-hauled on the port tack must keep clear of one close-hauled on the starboard tack," Maggie recited. "I can't think which tack is which, at least not fast enough. I'm going to run into somebody."

"Don't worry. If you do, you've got a lawyer on board."

"What if I don't have a lawyer on board?" Maggie asked, and there was a sudden, stricken silence.

Maria was in mid-Bay, dancing along in a light breeze, more or less sailing herself. It was a glorious day, with a hundred jaunty sailboats, many with brilliantly colored spinnakers, scattered on the calm water. The city, looking washed and polished, shone in the sun, like a treasure at the end of the rainbow. The fog had retreated to the western horizon.

Maggie glanced over her shoulder at the Golden Gate Bridge and gasped. "What's that?"

Under the bridge, from out of the fog, was coming something huge and bullet-shaped and dead black, and at enormous speed.

Peter turned to look. Maggie shivered.

"It's a nuclear submarine," Peter said.

The black brute plowed relentlessly through the water in a straight line toward Oakland, and there was no question as to who had the right-of-way. Sailboats scattered as it came, and then, with some herd instinct, tried to follow it, but to no avail. They were left bobbing in its wake.

As it passed *Maria*, a hundred yards away, Maggie saw that there was a small bridge and a conning tower atop the dead-black steel bullet, and that flags were flying from it. But there was no one on the bridge. There was nothing living. There was nothing moving. It churned onward, a blind black intruder on the happy playground of pretty little sailboats.

For Maggie, the sun seemed to dim. The colors faded and became washed out. The wind dropped, and *Maria* was making no headway at all. Without a word, Peter started the engine, and they took *Maria* back to the berth in Sausalito.

When they had stowed everything away, Peter said, "We have to talk."

"I know," said Maggie.

* * *

The bar at Scoma's had huge windows that overlooked Richardson Bay and the city, but it still managed to seem dim and secluded. Since it was only early afternoon, the bar was nearly empty. Peter ordered a Scotch and water, Maggie her usual standby wine, and waited for him to speak first.

"What did you think about when you saw that nuclear submarine?" he said.

"Terrible things, like what a frightening world we live in that we need to have war machines like that. There was no one on board. It seemed like a ghost ship." Maggie shuddered.

"There were plenty of people on board," Peter said. "They just never go on deck. They can go around the world underwater. Isn't that ironic? To go around the world and never see a thing?"

Maggie couldn't resist adding, "From what I hear, people do that on cruise ships."

Peter chuckled and then sobered. "My reaction to it was this: I'd like to be sailing somewhere where there aren't any sinister black warships bearing down on me, reminding me of how dangerous the world has gotten. I doubt it there are any of those in Bora Bora."

"Mine is a little different," Maggie said. "My reaction is to try to change things so that there is no need for sinister black warships in Bora Bora or San Francisco Bay."

"How do you propose to do that?" One of Peter's eyebrows was raised, Maggie noticed. He didn't like what she was saying.

"Right out of the civics books," she said. "Work for the candidate of my choice. For whoever thinks of the best way to make nuclear submarines unnecessary, one way or another. That really brought it home to me. What I do is really important."

"Is everybody in politics as idealistic as you are?" Peter asked. "I doubt it."

"Sure, some of them are there for the power and money, and some of them get sidetracked when they get into office, but a lot are good people who hate the thought of having to have nuclear subs, too."

"But you can do a lot more influencing than I can, considering what you do. All I have is one vote." Peter smiled at last.

"But you can stick around and vote. You can't vote in Bora Bora."

"Sure I can," Peter explained. "By absentee ballot."

"You're begging the question," Maggie said. "The point is, do you leave or do you stay around and fight to change things?"

"Maggie, how does Charles Portnoy feel about nuclear submarines?"

Maggie had to confess she didn't know.

"How about Bill Sutter?"

Maggie didn't know that, either. But if his point was that she was for Portnoy but didn't know his position on that single issue, she did know his positions generally and she approved. Sutter was not that much different, anyway. She would be very sorry if Portnoy lost, but she could live with Sutter.

"Then why bother?" Peter asked. "If there's no difference between candidates, why bother?"

"Because I believe that Portnoy is the better man," Maggie said, stung. "Because I think he can implement *my* ideas better. Because the American system is an adversary system, where people are given a choice. Because that's democracy. For that matter, why bother with what you do? Rincon Oil isn't a good cause, and neither is Leon Dickens."

"We've been over that before. Good cause, bad cause, I'm paid to make sure the acquisition, if it happens, is legal. And that in itself is good."

"May I have another glass of wine?" Maggie asked, suddenly tired of this discussion, which seemed to be leading nowhere.

"Sure," he said, and signaled the waitress.

"Peter, who is Maria?"

"Nobody," he told her.

There was, or so they each believed, a yawning chasm between them. Peter could not have known that Maggie went home that night thinking that, despite her brave words, she wasn't doing very much to preserve democracy and make the world safe from warships. Neither Portnoy nor Sutter could do very much about them, either. So what did it matter? And what did it matter what means you used to gain a good? It must be nice to be a lawyer, she thought, and only have to deal with legalities, not right and wrong. Probably he was right. It was all a waste of time anyway, when way out there was Bora Bora, the exact latitude and longitude of which she knew, and where there were no nuclear submarines. She would go with Peter, or he would go with Maria, whoever she was, or Maggie would go by herself. She would vote in American Samoa, the exact latitude and longitude of which she also knew.

Nor could Maggie have known what Peter was thinking: that Maggie was right, that sailing to Bora Bora was a cop-out, and that he could do more about nuclear submarines by staying here. That maybe his approach was too legalistic, that he should start making some moral judgments. Sailing on the Bay wasn't as good as sailing around the world, but it would do, and maybe he could buy a bigger boat and enter the TransPac race, which only took six months, or maybe just sail to Hawaii, as dull as that sounded.

But the main thing was, he didn't think he could leave Maggie. That whole conversation had gotten off on the wrong track because what he'd been leading up to was trying to convince her to go with him. Good thing he hadn't finished. She'd made it very clear that her feet were rooted in the concrete. Not that it was bad concrete; it was good, honest, idealistic concrete. Could he give up his dream for her? He decided it would be the noble thing to do. And San Francisco, after all, wasn't too bad. He'd seen worse.

At the door, Peter broke all the rules and kissed Maggie good-night. It took each of them several hours to recover from it, in their respective apartments.

Chapter Ten

Maggie plunged back into her killer schedule. She wrote another mailer for Carol Gold, suggested door-to-door canvassing for Harley Davis, talked to people about precious TV time for Portnoy. In the last two weeks they would spend as much as they could on TV spots. The office computer was going into overload and acting up. Ted was more churlish than usual. Fred Oliver made snide remarks, usually out of Portnoy's hearing. Three months into the campaign, they were already a month behind. Maggie tried to think of synonyms for that condition somewhere between "chaos" and "mayhem."

Again breaking the rules, Maggie spent an evening that week watching TV with Peter in his apartment. And with Genghis Khat trying to come between them, and succeeding, Maggie was exhausted. When she fell asleep in the middle of Ted Koppel, Peter knew how tired she was and took her home.

"On Sunday, I'm taking you away from all this," Peter said.

"Where?" Maggie asked.

"My surprise," he said, and grinned, rumpling her already rumpled hair.

Sunday morning, when Peter turned north and went across the Golden Gate Bridge, Maggie still had little idea of where they might be going. It was not until he turned east at the top of the Bay that she figured it out. "The Napa Valley," she exclaimed.

"Right on. What's your favorite winery?"

"Falconcrest," Maggie answered immediately.

Peter groaned and drove on.

They stopped, as every pilgrim to the Napa Valley must, at one of the wineries, this one modern Spanish mission-style. It sat dead center in the finest wine-growing area on earth, its rows of grapevines stretching to the foot of the mountains that enclosed the valley. Like all wineries, it offered free wine-tasting, but that came at the end of a tour. Maggie had been on these tours a dozen times, but Peter hadn't. He was totally absorbed in the great steel tanks, the oaken barrels, the talk of acidity and "sitting on the skins" and Ph counts and bottling. Maggie took this opportunity to pursue her own personal interests: she watched Peter. He looked particularly fine today, she thought. He was wearing a yellow polo shirt and white pants, which with his blond hair and his tan ought to have made him look like an L.A. surfer. But some-

how it didn't. She tried to decide which feature in his
face she liked best: the tawny eyes, the wide mouth,
the dimple when he smiled. She'd mentioned that
dimple once, and both his eyebrows had gone up—he
hadn't liked that at all. That thick, streaked blond hair
was very nice, especially the way it came to a V at the
back of his neck.

"Is something wrong?" Peter had caught her staring at his neck.

"No, not a thing," Maggie said.

He put a casual hand on her shoulder and continued listening to the tour guide.

Maggie thought she couldn't be happier, with this
man, in this beautiful place, on this sunny day. But
suddenly a cold shiver ran down her spine, out of nowhere. It would not always be like this. They'd done
a good job of not thinking about the inevitable part-
ing of the ways that lay ahead, but with every day,
sunny or foggy, the day approached. Like that black
submarine.

Peter noticed the shiver and looked down at her in
concern.

"Too much refrigeration," Maggie explained.

But now they were in the salesroom, where small
glasses of several varieties of wine were being poured
out and offered to the visitors. Peter got two glasses of
a dark red cabernet, the specialty of this winery, and
handed one to Maggie.

"May you always get the jib on right side up," he
said.

"Are you ever going to forget that?" Maggie asked
plaintively.

"No."

Maggie changed the subject. "What do you think of the wine?"

Peter swirled it in his glass, sniffed it, swirled it again, took a small sip, held it in his mouth for a while, swallowed and said, "Presumptuous."

"It's got a big nose."

"A little corky."

"Stemmy."

"I can't think of any more adjectives."

"More adjectives than wine. Let's go somewhere else."

The highway, California 29, meandered northward through the green and sun-drenched valley, past wineries with famous names designed to look like medieval castles, Victorian mansions, fifteenth-century monasteries, Bauhaus art galleries, Swiss chalets. Peter drove until they reached the sleepy little town of Calistoga, at the northern end, where he treated Maggie to a sumptuous lunch, replete with wine. Then he said, "Where is it?" as they walked out the door.

"Where is what?" asked Maggie, blinking in the bright sun. She felt like curling up under a shady tree and taking a nap.

"You'll see. It's what I brought you up here for." He was looking up and down the sidewalk on the main street.

"What is it?" Maggie said, almost annoyed. This was her only day off, and she didn't want to be dragged around some little town in the September heat.

"Look at this," Peter insisted. A small plaque on the side of a stone building explained how Calistoga had gotten its name. It seems that it was to have been named Saratoga, after the spa in New York. However, the senator who dedicated the town introduced it as "Calistoga, Sarafornia" and the name stuck.

"That's funny," said Maggie without much enthusiasm. She turned and walked right into Fred Oliver.

"Maggie, what are you doing here?" said Fred.

"I honestly don't know," Maggie answered, feeling her heart sink into her shoes. "Just up for the day. How about you?"

"Me, too. Going to the mud baths." He looked with frank curiosity at Peter, who was standing quietly behind Maggie.

"Fred, this is Peter Barnes. Peter, Fred Oliver," Maggie didn't know if Fred knew who Peter Barnes was, but she wanted to be sure Peter knew who Fred was, so she added, "He's Charles Portnoy's campaign chairman."

She no longer felt like curling up and taking a nap. Now her mind was racing. Of all the people to run into when she was with Peter, Fred Oliver was the worst. He knew everybody, or if he didn't, he could find out with one phone call.

There was some polite small talk, and Fred went off down the sidewalk.

"Oh, Lord," said Maggie. "Now I'm in hot water."

"He won't know who I am. I'm not exactly conspicuous in the Sutter campaign."

"He'll find out."

"Well, if he does, there's no harm done. We have never ever discussed the campaign, have we?"

"That's true."

"Well, I'll testify to that."

"It'll never get that far." Maggie sighed. "Close proximity is enough."

"There's nothing you can do about it, so let's go," Peter said, taking her hand.

"Now will you tell me what it is you are looking for? Before I sit down in the street and scream?"

"The mud baths, just like Mr. Oliver."

"No," said Maggie in horror. "No mud baths. I am not a water buffalo."

"Yes," said Peter very firmly. "We just have to make sure Fred Oliver isn't in the one we pick."

A few minutes later, Maggie found herself lying stark naked in a large bathtublike container full of hot brown mud—actually volcanic lava and peat moss, heated by mineral spring water. Only her head stuck out, and it rested on a strange little pillow. She was in the center of a huge tiled room, and the other tub of mud was empty. This was the women's side of the baths. Soft-voiced attendants hovered. Maggie wondered at first if this was because victims had been known to sink under the mud and disappear forever. But she had to admit it *felt* wonderful, no matter how ridiculous it must look.

After ten minutes in the mud, she never wanted to get out again, but at the attendant's insistence she pulled herself out and was hosed off before she got to the shower. Then she was Jacuzzied, blanketed, given iced mineral water, massaged with almond oil, dressed, propped on her feet and helped out the door. There was not a nerve or muscle or bone left in her body.

Peter was waiting for her, looking fresh and brisk. "I guess I am a water buffalo, after all." Maggie grinned, though even grinning took a Herculean effort. "You take me to the nicest places. How'd you know about the mud baths?"

"Guidebook," Peter said. "And it was retaliation for the elephant seals. Can you make it to the car? Or do you want to be carried?"

Maggie wanted to be carried more than life itself, but the idea of Fred Oliver seeing that sight was too horrifying. So she walked on rubbery legs the intervening blocks to the car, and by loosening her seat belt she managed to fall asleep on Peter's shoulder.

It was long after dark when Maggie woke up, realizing the car had stopped. Peter was gently shaking her. She opened her eyes, sat up, and looked through the windshield. Peter had turned from Highway 101 onto the narrow road on the Marin Headlands on the north side of the Golden Gate, five hundred feet above the water. The great red bridge was below them, its deck a streak of moving headlights. The grand art deco towers, softly lighted, soared above the dark tides of the Golden Gate. Beyond it lay the city, a fairyland of lights. Every time she saw this view and that bridge, Maggie felt like crying. She could barely believe that she was lucky enough to live in that beautiful place. And the bridge, that incredibly graceful span, the bridge was the beacon that lighted the way home.

"You've got tears in your eyes," Peter said. "What's the matter?"

"Nothing's the matter," Maggie said, brushing them away with the back of her hand. "It's just so beautiful. It's where I live. I could never leave."

Peter was silent all the way home.

Maggie fell into bed and was asleep in thirty seconds. She didn't even bother to look at the flashing red light on her answering machine, which meant that there were messages for her.

Chapter Eleven

In the morning Maggie woke up early, before the alarm went off, and felt wonderful. She could tackle anything, she thought, even the week that was coming up. She was a big fan of mud baths, she decided as she took a long shower. She put on a black skirt, an oversize black sweater and her fuzzy pink bedroom slippers, made a pot of coffee and took some croissants out of the freezer and microwaved them. That would have horrified her mother, Maggie thought, but as far as she was concerned, the microwave oven was the greatest invention since frozen lobster Newburg, which also would have horrified her mother.

She looked at her kitchen clock. Still really early. She could read both the Sunday paper, which she'd missed, and today's. Maggie was a news junkie. One thing she liked about Peter was that he had a subscription to the *Wall Street Journal* and she could read that, too, when she was at his place.

A delicious morning, she thought, looking out toward the cloudless horizon and opening the front section of the *Chronicle*. On page 4 of the Sunday paper was a picture of Peter, identified as "finance chairman of the Sutter campaign." It wasn't really a picture of Peter per se, but of a well-known eastern senator who had come to San Francisco to endorse Sutter and attend a hundred-dollar-a-plate banquet at the Fairmont Hotel for his benefit. Peter happened to be standing on one side of the senator and Sutter on the other.

Maggie had known about this gala event, of course, and had thought it a mistake to bring in out-of-state celebrities for congressional endorsements. She studied the picture and read the article. The senator was clearly setting himself up to run for president in four years. He had made a major foreign-policy speech.

Maggie was willing to bet that the senator had lost votes for Sutter. San Franciscans were a breed unto themselves. In fact, the *Chronicle* and the *Examiner* regularly accused them of being so independent that they were no longer part of the United States. Sutter should have known that. And, most especially, his campaign consultant should have known. But his campaign consultants were a famous Los Angeles firm, and if San Francisco was no longer part of the United States, Los Angeles was on another planet entirely. He should have used someone local; Maggie could have told him that.

Then it dawned on Maggie that if Fred Oliver hadn't known who Peter was, he did now. Fred didn't miss a thing, and he had one person working for him who did nothing but follow the Sutter campaign. The jig, as they said, was up. It probably wouldn't make any difference, but when Maggie went on to page 5 of the paper, she wasn't quite as happy as she had been before she'd seen that picture.

And it wasn't until an hour and three cups of coffee later that she saw the flashing light on the answering machine.

She put the tape on rewind and then played it. Fred Oliver wanted to talk to her at once. As soon as she got in from Calistoga.

When Maggie reached the office, Ted was standing in the door with a list.

"Don't even sit down," he said. "You have to decide right now on how many bumper stickers you want, that graphic artist you hired to lay out the Davis mailers is spaced out somewhere, three files of key supporters have disappeared off the data base, you have to farm out that newspaper ad and do the copy, and Fred Oliver's been calling here every five minutes. And you're late."

Maggie snapped, "Fifty thousand, call another one from that list, retrieve them, I'll do it today, and let him call."

Ted looked impressed. "Right on top of it today, aren't we?" The phone began its shrill ringing.

"And I'm not late, either," Maggie said, stepping around Ted and reaching for the phone. "Hello, Fred."

Fred didn't even bother to say hello. "You and that Barnes guy must be pretty good friends, going to the Napa Valley and all, right?"

"Pretty good," Maggie said cautiously.

"How long've you known this guy?"

"Not long, but it's none of your business, Fred." Maggie sat down and slipped off her shoes, feeling as if she were going into battle. But the battle was not to be the one that she expected.

"I presume that if you were associating with somebody from the other camp, you were exchanging information, right?"

"Wrong," Maggie said flatly.

"Then I can presume that what you had in mind for our candidate was to obtain information about their candidate, right?"

"Wrong."

"I see. Well, maybe you can start now. I'd hate to have to get a new consultant at this stage, but it can be done."

"Are you threatening me?" Maggie said sweetly.

"Yes," Fred said, just as pleasantly.

"Does Portnoy know about this?" Maggie asked.

"No, and I hope he doesn't find out. He's very fond of you. He would feel betrayed. That's not a good feeling when you're getting to the end of a hot campaign. Now, I hope you get that good intelligence just coming right in. We're most interested in their television campaign, but you know that."

"Fred?"

"What?"

"Stick it in your ear!"

* * *

For the first time, Maggie called Peter at his office. "Meet me at Hennessey's downstairs after work," she commanded.

"Isn't that risky?"

"Nobody political goes there, and it's dark."

"I may be a little late."

"That's okay. I can wait."

"Who was that?" Ted asked from his position over the keyboard of the computer as she hung up the phone.

"Polling. They wanted to know who I was voting for in the Fifth District."

Maggie had previously arranged four focus groups to test some theories she and Ted had about the images of Charles Portnoy and William Sutter. These voter discussion groups had identified a number of problems for both sides. Sutter was considered aloof, something of an outsider, despite his name and probably incorruptible because of his money. His positions were perceived as not much different from Portnoy's, with a couple of exceptions: law and order and taxes. Sutter was the trim three-piece-suiter, the Montgomery Street lawyer, who spoke well, seemed honest and intelligent and had a very famous name. Portnoy was the rumpled bear who looked as if he had gravy on his tie even when he didn't. Portnoy's image was of the hometown boy, someone who lived in "the neighborhood"—which he did—and did a very good job, but was very much a political animal, a power broker.

Using this information, Maggie spent a long afternoon with the media consultant and a representative of the ad agency working out the basics of the television spots, which would be shown only in the last two weeks of the campaign. There wasn't that much money, and they had sacrificed a lot—a direct-mail campaign, radio—in order to do it. They decided that one would show Portnoy coming out the front door of his modest house on his way to work and talking with his neighbors about what he would do in Washington for them.

"Slice of life," Maggie said. "I'll bet you can use the real neighbors."

"That way we leave it to the imagination of the viewers as to just how big Sutter's St. Francis' Wood mansion is," said the media consultant.

"How big is it?" Maggie asked.

"I don't know, but I bet it's bigger than mine."

"Now all we need is Portnoy's okay."

"And Fred Oliver, don't forget."

"Who's the media buyer?"

And the rest of the afternoon was spent on the endless details, with talk of rating points and storyboards until well after five. Maggie raced—as much as you could race in that elevator—to the ground floor and into Hennessey's through the grimy side door. She looked around in the gloom, failed to see Peter and sought out an empty table. She waved off the cocktail waitress and put her chin in her hands and gazed glumly at the door.

It was a full hour before Peter showed up, and as he stood in the doorway, looking for Maggie, she thought that he could stand in for Sutter in *their* television spots. The three-piece suit was there, perfectly tailored, the subdued tie, the thirty-dollar haircut and even the bulging but excellent leather lawyer's briefcase. Cookie-cutter lawyers, she thought, cookie-cutter Yalies. She stopped herself short. What was this? Was *she* beginning to think of Peter as the enemy?

He made his way over to the table, and in the process became the familiar, beloved Peter.

"What's up?" he said, stowing his briefcase under the table and sliding into a chair. "You don't look very happy."

"I'm not. Fred Oliver's blackmailing me."

"He's *what*?" Peter leaned forward, concern in his eyes.

"Unless I get information on the Sutter campaign from you and give it to him, he'll get me fired."

The tawny eyes turned steely, and the square jaw became even squarer. "That SOB."

"I think we'd better stop seeing each other until this is over," Maggie said.

"I disagree," Peter replied. "That wouldn't help anyway. You couldn't prove you hadn't seen me. Rule in law: you can't prove a negative. You're the best thing in my life right now. I don't..." His voice trailed off. Then he added, "But my problems have nothing to do with it."

"It's only for a month or so," Maggie said, but there wasn't much conviction in her voice.

"What kind of intelligence information does he want?"

"I shouldn't tell you this, but we know almost everything about Sutter's campaign, except the TV spots."

"How did you get that information? Not from me."

"Fred has people who do nothing but follow the Sutter campaign and second-guess it."

"What if you told the despicable Mr. Oliver that I didn't have the information he needed?" Peter said. "I hold the purse strings, that's all, and I haven't paid that much attention to the rest of it. Of course, I hope Bill wins, but I'm a figurehead. I wanted it that way."

"What if the Sutter campaign finds out about you and me?" Maggie hadn't thought of that before.

"If they cared, I'd resign. I don't do it for a living, like you do. But I don't think it would make much difference. Bill Sutter already knows there's a smashing redhead that sails with me."

"He does?" Maggie was surprised, but not too surprised to file away that "smashing."

"He saw you out there on Opening Day. He sails, too. He used the word 'smashing,' by the way. Not that I wouldn't, too."

"What did you tell him?" Maggie was intrigued.

"That you were somebody I'd met at Rick's." He grinned. "I wouldn't do you in. You wanted it secret, I kept it secret."

"So what do you think I should do?" Maggie said. "Be my legal counsel."

"I think you should go on doing what you've been doing. Seeing me when you damn please. And you can truthfully tell Mr. Oliver that I don't know anything about the TV campaign, or anything else except the finances, and that I'll say that in court if I have to. Does that sound all right to you?"

Peter's certainty gave Maggie confidence. "It sounds fine. Thank you, Peter." She reached over and put her hand over his, and he captured it and held it tight. A warm glow suffused her.

"Now," said Peter, signaling the waitress with his free hand, "let's have a drink and figure out what we'll do Sunday. Do you want to go sailing or sailing?"

"I think sailing," Maggie said happily.

As it turned out, it was a week before the mud hit the fan.

Chapter Twelve

Exactly three weeks before election day, the Sutter television spots were first broadcast. They were able to buy the best of all times, immediately after the local news, both at six and eleven. And, of course, they were on all three major channels and several minor ones. This much Maggie could have guessed. That was what anyone with a lot of money would do. She also guessed that these would be "less positive" than Portnoy's, due to the Los Angeles campaign consultants. The farther south you went in California, the dirtier the campaigns. But she was not prepared for what she did see.

Everyone involved in Portnoy's campaign full-time—by now nearly fifty people, many of them volunteers—had gathered in the former car dealership with the huge Portnoy for Congress posters on the windows. Good color TVs had been brought in, and

VCRs to record these one-minute events. There was still time to change the spots for Portnoy, which wouldn't run for another week. It would be tough, but it could be done. While the news ran, there was a good deal of talk and a good deal of fiddling with VCRs by their owners.

"You'd think this was the opening of the opera," someone near Maggie said. They were all standing or leaning on tables or desks. Only Charles Portnoy was sitting on a chair, right in front, looking like a shaggy mountain.

Maggie was only a little sunburned from yesterday's sailing, which had consisted of a hundred man-overboard drills, and only a little tired.

Furthermore, Maggie thought, she had been able to escape from the clutches of Fred Oliver all week. She would not answer his phone calls, and she had managed not to be in a room alone with him. She made sure there were at least ten other people. And the chief pieces of intelligence he wanted, the TV spots, were coming on in less than a minute, the actual thing. He couldn't want anything else from her.

But now Dave and Wendy were saying good-night to each other, the station logo and the network logo came on, then faded out, and on the screen came another newscaster. For a moment Maggie thought it was Jim Whitten, a local anchorman, but she realized it was not. It was an actor who looked very much like him. He was sitting behind the standard newscaster's desk, and behind him was the ubiquitous screen, with a huge picture of William Sutter. At the top of the screen, in very small letters, there appeared the words

Paid Political Advertisement. They vanished almost instantly. Maggie wasn't even sure she'd seen them.

"Candidate for Congress William Sutter announced today that his first major piece of legislation after he is seated in Congress will be aimed at strengthening the war on drug dealers, who are destroying the fabric of American society. The president has personally promised Sutter the utmost support in this vitally important legislation."

Sutter disappeared, and there was a brief shot of the president smiling benignly. Then the president faded, and two pictures came on the screen behind the newscaster. One was a very unflattering shot of Charles Portnoy, and the other was of a notorious Colombian cocaine czar who had recently been arrested in a raid. He was pictured in handcuffs, averting his face from the camera, surrounded by stern men with guns. Underneath was lettered: Portnoy votes *for* drugs. The announcer intoned, "It was learned recently that William Sutter's opponent, Charles Portnoy, is on record as having voted for the legalization of controlled substances. Had he been successful, men such as Carlos Baumann would be free today to wreak their terrible havoc on our children." The newscaster paused long enough for every viewer to get a good look at Portnoy and Baumann, and then a smiling Sutter appeared again. "We recommend a vote for William Sutter for Congress, Fifth District." Fade-out.

There was a stunned and sickened silence.

Fred Oliver was the first to speak. His face was blotchy and red. "Anybody know what that's all about?"

"I presume they're talking about my sponsorship of that proposition to decriminalize marijuana possession—not dealing—in the city," Portnoy said. "It was to bring the city law into line with state law. Years ago. But I agreed with it."

Maggie remembered. Ten years ago the voters had passed a ballot proposition making possession of less than an ounce of marijuana less than a misdemeanor. The penalty was the equivalent of a traffic ticket. This had freed law-enforcement officials to go after the big dealers and growers, where their time was better spent.

"If you liked that," someone else said, "you'll love what was on channel 5. Look at this." He switched on the VCR.

Same announcer, same format, but this time Portnoy was shown with Yasir Arafat. As a member of the Airport Commission he had voted against some security equipment that he'd deemed too expensive for the marginal increase in safety it promised. Therefore, Portnoy encouraged hijackers and terrorists.

Channel 7 showed Portnoy disarming America while the Soviet hordes poured over the border. Portnoy had voted to ban handguns in the city, as had the vast majority of the voting population.

"There's more coming up at eleven," the media buyer said.

"I'm sick to my stomach," said a woman. "I didn't think that was done anymore."

"It's a revival," said Maggie ironically. "Like art deco."

"Very funny." Fred Oliver looked right at her. "You have a few things to answer for."

Maggie looked over at Charles Portnoy. He was smiling wryly. "Okay, kiddies, I think it's time to go home. At least they didn't find out that I was beating my wife and kicking my dog." He lumbered up out of his seat. "It'll all look better in the morning."

"I think we should have a meeting right now," Fred Oliver said. "We can't waste any time countering this."

Portnoy loomed over him. "I said, we go home. Sleep on it. Tomorrow, 8:00 a.m., breakfast at the Gavel, we'll talk about it."

Maggie went home, half sick, half furious. When Peter called that night, she was short with him, then called him back and apologized. She advised him to watch the eleven o'clock news. He said he already planned to.

The meeting the following morning was worse than Maggie had expected, and she had expected the worst. The Gavel was a smoke-filled room with a bar and grill across the street from the courthouse, and it was always full of the kind of people who hung around courthouses: lawyers in cheap suits with cardboard attaché cases, bail bondsmen. But it had terrific breakfasts. Maggie ordered bacon, two eggs over easy, hash browns, orange juice, an English muffin and coffee. It was, she figured, her last meal. She remembered what Peter had said and smiled to herself.

Maybe I should order a cigarette and a blindfold, she thought. Fred Oliver was going to line her up against the wall and shoot her.

There was just the three of them there: Maggie, Oliver, Portnoy.

"Tell me again about last week's numbers," Portnoy said, looking at Maggie.

"It's 43 for you, 45 for Sutter and 2 percent for None of the Above. That leaves ten percent in the undecided column," she told him. "I think those commercials mean he's running scared."

"When can we get another poll?"

"To see the effect of those ads? A week." Maggie said.

"And that's too late to change anything," Fred Oliver interjected. "Whatever we do, we've got to decide now. And I don't think they're putting those things out because they're running scared. I think it was the plan all along. That firm that's working for him is famous for campaigns like that."

"I think it will backfire," Maggie insisted. "That firm is from Los Angeles, where things like that work. It won't work here."

"It won't work?" Fred Oliver smiled nastily. "That firm, as you called it, got two presidents elected."

Maggie smiled sweetly. "That firm, as I called it, didn't get them elected in northern California. Northern California went for the other guy both times."

Portnoy interrupted them. "So you are going to recommend, Maggie, on the basis of no polls whatsoever, that we do nothing?"

Maggie didn't like the sound of that, but she nodded. "Turn the other cheek, I think it's called."

"And you, Fred? You say strike back?"

"Yep. We can the nice neighborhood commercials and do something slick, like the Sutter ads, using that Yale transcript." Fred poured more syrup over his stack of pancakes. They were already floating. Maggie's stomach churned a little at the sight.

"Maybe we could even dig up some more. Maggie here has a way to do it. Don't you, Maggie?"

"I don't know what you mean, Fred." Maggie buttered her English muffin, waiting for the revelation.

"Maggie here has been carrying on...a relationship with a close friend of Sutter's. They were classmates at Yale, now they're partners in the same law firm, and this guy, Barnes, is mixed up in the Sutter campaign. He's finance chairman."

Portnoy looked up from his waffle. "You're seeing him right now, Maggie? During the campaign?"

Maggie nodded. "I swear that we agreed not to discuss the slightest thing about it, and we haven't. I have never given him any information, nothing. And he hasn't given me any."

"I find that hard to believe," Fred Oliver said. "It would be impossible not to talk about what you were doing with somebody you were that close to. In fact, I might even suggest that Maggie's reluctance to use the Yale transcript has something to do with protecting her good friend, whose good friend is Bill Sutter. Come clean, Maggie. Where do your loyalties lie?"

Maggie stood up, nearly overturning the table and spilling everyone's coffee. She reached in her purse and threw a five-dollar bill on the table.

"I will not have my integrity questioned, by you or anyone else. I quit. I'm sorry, Mr. Portnoy, I really want you to win, but I can't do it Fred's way. It's not right."

"Right or wrong has nothing to do with it," Fred said with a note of what Maggie thought might be glee in his voice.

Maggie turned on her heel and started toward the door.

"Maggie, wait," Portnoy said.

But Fred Oliver said, louder, "All's fair in love and war, Maggie." Maggie thought he sounded triumphant. And very much like someone she knew, namely Peter.

Maggie took a cab to the office, told Ted to bundle up everything they had on Portnoy and messenger it to Fred Oliver's office. Finding somebody to do all those jobs would give Fred some pause, but not much. Most of it was done, except the daily polling they had planned for the last two weeks. And he could hire the same pollster she did.

That still left Maggie with Carol Gold and Harley Davis, but beyond some radio spots and a closely targeted mailing for the former and a phone bank for the latter, there was little left to do for either. She told Ted he could have some time off, and that she wasn't accepting any phone calls. Then she locked herself in the ladies' room down the hall and cried for an hour, and when she got back to her office, she called Peter and asked him to meet her early for dinner. Someplace nice and public, she thought, but Peter couldn't make it for dinner that night. He was busy. This she learned from him after going through two secretaries.

That night, Portnoy called her at home.

"You sure you want to resign, Maggie?"

She was sure. She could not work with Fred Oliver, but she didn't say that aloud.

Portnoy told her he believed in her integrity, and that she'd done a wonderful job, and that he hoped she'd come to his victory party anyway, even if she wasn't still working on the campaign. Fairmont Hotel, top of Nob Hill.

"I will, I promise," she said. "If you don't mind me asking, have you decided on what to do about the transcript?"

Portnoy sighed. "I don't know. We don't have any polling set up yet to learn what we should do."

"Polling, schmolling," Maggie told him. "Go with your heart."

"I'll remember that, Maggie. Thanks."

It was three days before Peter was able to meet her for dinner, and by that time Maggie was beginning to think he was avoiding her. Nor did even the phone conversation get off to an auspicious start.

"Where do you want to go to dinner?"

"I don't know. Someplace good."

"Well, what do you want to eat?"

"How about Chinese?"

"I had Chinese yesterday. There's a new Persian restaurant in my neighborhood. Shall we try that?"

"Actually, I was thinking Vietnamese."

"I'd prefer Ethiopian."

"Turkish?"

"Greek."

"French."

"Italian."

"I *really* don't care!"

They finally settled on Cajun, probably, Maggie thought, because Peter was being so fastidiously yuppie. She could hear his three-piece suit over the phone. It was saying, "Cajun's in, Cajun's in."

The Louisiana Café, which they had to wait half an hour to get into, was decorated in 1930s Depression style in a beautiful 1870s building. It was in SOMA, meaning it was South of Market Street, an area of warehouses and wholesalers. SOMA was "coming back," coming back so fast that Maggie was afraid it would turn into a giant boutique overnight, as other districts had. A year ago SOMA had been a place to stay away from at night. Now it held restaurants that had mannequins' legs coming out of the walls or fake inkstains on the floor, and comedy clubs in dark basements. SOMA was even more "in" than Cajun food.

It was a requirement of the place to have the specialty of the house, blackened redfish. Maggie tried to avoid it, but there was little alternative. Resigned to her fate, she ordered it and then asked for a large glass of water. She had been to Cajun places before.

After the waiter left, Peter said, "What's this all about? Should we be seen in public?"

"The cover's blown, Peter. Fred Oliver tattled."

"I'm glad. So that's over." Peter seemed distracted.

"I'm over, too," Maggie told him.

"What does that mean?" Now he looked concerned.

"It means that I don't have the Portnoy account anymore. I quit."

"How do you feel about that?" Peter asked. "I thought you liked him."

"I feel good and bad about it. I feel good because I did the right thing and I feel bad because it probably set me back two years in my business. It was the biggest job I ever had, and I couldn't handle it."

"Why did you quit?"

"Did you see the Sutter spots? On TV?"

"Yeah."

"What did you think?"

"Well, I thought they were very well done, technically. They should be, for what we paid the agency."

"Peter, I mean what did you think of the content?"

"Well, it was grammatical."

"Don't be so deliberately dense."

Peter shrugged. "They were just political ads. What more can I say?"

"Did you see them beforehand? Did you know what was in them?"

"Maggie, I have been so busy on the Rincon thing that I haven't even had time to sign the checks for the campaign. No, I didn't see them beforehand."

At that point the tossed salad arrived. Maggie figured it was safe to eat it and took a large forkful. She burst into tears.

"Water," she gasped. "Hand me the water."

Peter handed her the glass, and after she drank it all she sat back in her chair, wiping the tears with her napkin.

"You've got to be more careful," Peter advised her. "They put hot sauce in everything."

Maggie ate the rest of her salad in tiny bites, after Peter ordered another glass of water for her. It was hell. She was hungry, and couldn't bear to put the food in her mouth. She attacked the bread, fearing to put butter on it, as she reasoned it might be adulterated with hot sauce.

When the entree came, Maggie decided that it looked like a burnt fish, which was what it was. By peeling off the top half inch of the fish, she was able to eat what remained—the pepper could not penetrate that far. The baked potato was safe as long as she didn't put anything on it, but when she tried the vegetables she had to reach for the water again, with flames, she was sure, coming from her ears.

"Now explain all this to me again," Peter said. "You lost me back there. What did those TV spots have to do with your quitting?"

Maggie told him. "You don't realize that was a negative campaign, as they so nicely put it?"

"Of course I recognized it. Not nice at all."

"And it doesn't bother you?"

"Why should it? It's just another campaign tactic, isn't it? Can't we just assume that Portnoy will do the same thing? Isn't it done all the time?"

"You mean you really believe that 'All's fair in love and war'?" Maggie was outraged. "You and Fred Oliver both quoted that at me. You really thought that was the way things should be done in a political campaign?"

"Do you remember Opening Day, talking about the Rincon acquisition?" Peter said. "Politics and the law are the same there, it seems to me. There isn't any 'ought to be' or 'should be,' there just is what there is. You do what you have to do to win."

"You believe that. No moral judgments, you said, didn't you?"

"I said, not in the law."

"And not in political campaigns, according to you."

"Maggie, don't get me wrong. Those TV spots were legal, they were accepted practice. There are plenty of illegal things you can do in a political campaign, and the laws are on the books. You can't slip twenty-dollar bills to voters outside the polls, you can't tamper with voting machines, you can't intimidate people. That's the law—collective moral judgments. There's no law against dirty campaign ads."

Maggie now felt that, instead of fire, there was steam coming out of her ears.

"Do you know why I quit?" she nearly yelled. "I quit because Fred Oliver wanted to counter those ads with some nasty stuff we have on Sutter. I didn't want to have anything to do with it. And he wanted me to try to get more out of you."

"What nasty stuff?" Peter said, sitting up straight. "What do you have on Bill?"

"The Yale transcript," Maggie said without thinking, and then considered suicide. The three words were hanging in the air between them like a cartoon balloon. She should never have said it, never. It was a campaign secret, it was Portnoy's to use or not, and now she had tipped off the opposition.

The waiter appeared at her elbow and momentarily distracted them with the dessert menu. Maggie ordered vanilla ice cream, and Peter asked for pecan pie and "Blackened coffee for both of us, please." Maggie refrained from laughing.

"Now—" Peter leaned across the table "—tell me, what Yale transcript?"

Maggie sighed. "Is there any chance I can get you to promise that you won't tell anybody else?"

"No, not now. Maybe later when I hear what it is."

"A few weeks ago an anonymous donor sent us a copy of Sutter's transcript at Yale. It showed that he had been suspended for a year because he had cheated."

"Well, that's a forgery, because I went all the way through Yale undergraduate and law school with Bill, and as far as I know he never cheated, and he certainly wasn't suspended, least of all for a year."

"It looked very authentic," Maggie said. "It had the embossed seal and all."

"You can fake anything nowadays." Peter stopped, lost in thought. "I wonder who sent it?"

"A friend, it said." Maggie looked hard at Peter. "Are you sure you aren't just covering for Sutter?"

"I'm sure. And I'll even promise you I won't tell anyone about it. Because now that you know it's fake you wouldn't dare use it."

Maggie sat up very straight. "Do *not*, repeat, do *not*, include me in that pronoun 'you.' I am the one who argued not to use it in the first place, and I am the one who quit because Fred Oliver still wanted to use it. I do not work for the campaign anymore, and I am not responsible if it is used, forgery or not."

"Maggie, it won't be used," Peter said. "If it is, we—Bill—can bat it down immediately with the real transcript. It would just rebound on Portnoy. Don't you see that?"

"You're wrong, dead wrong. Even if Fred Oliver knew it was fake, he would use it. And you know how? A big press conference, a television blitz, the day before the election. I repeat, the day before the election. Sutter couldn't do anything about it until afterward, but it would be too late. The votes would already be in."

"That would be really dirty pool. I'm surprised at you, Maggie. Knowing how to do things like that," Peter said. Maggie looked hard at him to see if he was being facetious. Evidently he wasn't.

"I know it because I am good at what I do. It's the oldest technique in the world. But that doesn't mean I'd use it."

"How much do you want Portnoy to win?" Peter asked.

"A lot," said Maggie.

Peter sighed. "If I were you, and still working on the campaign, and I thought it was real, I'd use it."

"And if you thought it was fake?" Maggie said nastily.

"Of course not," he said. "What do you take me for?"

Maggie, not knowing the answer to that question, finished her vanilla ice cream and her coffee, and after Peter had paid they walked drearily past the warehouses on the deserted streets to the car. Though they were side by side, there was a rift the size of the Grand Canyon between them.

Chapter Thirteen

And so, two weeks before the big election, the one Maggie had looked forward to all her life, she found herself without a job and without Peter. As far as the job was concerned, she still had some things to do for Harley Davis and Carol Gold, but not much. Harley was a shoo-in, a circumstance not really attributable to her work, and Carol was going to lose and had run out of money.

As far as Peter was concerned, Maggie knew she wouldn't hear from him again, and she was right. Her original instincts had been right—WASP lawyers and Irish pols' daughters didn't mix well. This time she couldn't be noble about it. She was plain miserable. And, having worked fourteen-hour days for the last six months, she didn't know what to do with herself.

She tried going to the office, but even Ted didn't have enough to do. And it would get worse. After the election there was nothing, nothing. She would have to think about drumming up some polling business, scrounging to stay alive.

Sunday, when she was sure Peter was sailing, she went to Fleishhacker's big indoor pool for a swim, and then she walked along Ocean Beach, stopping at Playland to look in the funhouse mirrors and eat an It's It, an ice-cream-cookie-and-chocolate concoction and then she walked up to the Sutro baths, with some idea of a steam bath and a massage, à la the mud baths. But it wasn't the same. The idea or the place. Still, at least it had taken up the long day and reminded her of her childhood.

On Monday, to her astonishment, a large—very large—check arrived from the Portnoy campaign. She had literally forgotten that she worked for money. He had probably let everyone else go: the printer, the TV time people, to pay her. It was nice, she thought. It was more than nice. Most candidates wouldn't have done that. She took it to the bank. She could go for a long time on that check. It was funny how money made you feel better.

After that, just for the looks of it, she kept regular office hours and indulged in her addiction. She stopped at the big newsstand on the corner, bought the *New York Times*, the *Washington Post*, the *Los Angeles Times*, the *Wall Street Journal* and sometimes the *Christian Science Monitor*, not to mention the local papers, the *Chronicle* and the *Examiner*. She read every one of them, following with special attention the national elections. She did the *Times* crossword, increasing her vocabulary by such words as haha—a buried fence—and nene—a Hawaiian bird. In the *Examiner* one day there was an "inside" article on the Portnoy campaign, and it was mentioned prominently that Maggie McGraw, consultant, had been "let go" for reasons of strategy. No new consultant had been hired. None were available. Oh, great, thought Maggie. At least it hadn't been on page one, above the fold.

And all the papers carried articles on what had happened to Rincon Oil. The *Wall Street Journal* even had an editorial on it, which seemed to conflict with the slant of the news article, but Maggie was by now used to its schizophrenia. It seemed that Dickens the raider had been rebuffed, and another gigantic oil company, in the guise of a "white knight," had taken the fainting and barely protesting Rincon into its corporate arms. So now, instead of seven sisters in the oil business, there were only six. And Peter was out of a job, too, Maggie thought. He, too, had been paid for a lot of work that had come to nothing. How sweetly ironic.

Nearly every night she had been going out, mostly to the movies, getting home in time for Ted Koppel, to whom she was more attached than ever. She refused to watch the local news for fear she'd see those awful Sutter commercials again. Nights that she didn't go out she found herself charting a round-the-world course, working out latitude and longitude on her map. She had touched at Cape Town and now wondered whether to strike straight across the Atlantic to lonely Tristan da Cunha or to follow the coast of Africa—the Skeleton Coast!—north to the Cape Verdes and across to Barbados. But there was Devil's Island—that must be gotten in. Then all the Caribbean islands, and the Panama Canal. But how did a small boat get through the Canal? She'd have to find out. Or maybe, the other way—around Cape Horn, all the way around South America. Did small boats ever go that way?

It was then she decided that she was crazy. She wasn't going around the world. But she did have enough money to go somewhere. She went to a travel agent and picked up brochures, mostly on Hawaii. Nowhere near Tahiti or Bora Bora or Fiji, or any of the other places on her route. She decided she would hang around until the election was over, go to the victory parties and then take off.

"Did you notice? Sutter's changed his ads on TV," Ted said to her one day.

"No, I didn't notice," Maggie said. "What are they now?"

"Oh, just Mom-and-apple-pie stuff. You know."

"I wonder why."

"I know why." Ted told her. "Their polling showed it was backfiring. Or at least not helping."

Maggie was astounded. "How do you know about their polls?"

"Do you know anything about computer hacking?" Ted said.

"No," Maggie said.

"Then I won't explain it," Ted said. "But that was a week ago, and now the polls are going back up."

"For Sutter, you mean."

"Yeah, now they're even again. The public has a very short memory. And there's still that hard-core ten percent undecided."

On the Thursday before election day it was announced that Charles Portnoy would hold an important news conference. It would be televised. It would be held on Monday, the day before the election. It was announced on Thursday so that it would hit the Friday newspapers, not the Saturday, which had the lowest readership.

Maggie already knew what was to be announced. Portnoy would reveal that William Sutter had been suspended for cheating at Yale. He was desperate. And it might work, she thought. It was not innuendo, like Sutter's ads. Somehow, cheating at Yale was worse than cheating at State U. Sutter couldn't counter, and Portnoy would win and, after the fact, be horrified that it was a fake transcript. Of course, he didn't know it was fake. Only Maggie did.

All day Friday and all day Saturday Maggie told herself it was none of her business. On Sunday she tried to call Portnoy and Fred Oliver, but couldn't locate them. She went to campaign headquarters, which was open and roaring, but neither one was there. Portnoy was giving two more speeches that day, his scheduler said. Maybe early Monday morning. She went and had dinner and then went to Portnoy's house. Nobody home. She sat on the front steps in the dark until eleven-thirty, when a car pulled up and a

weary Portnoy stepped out. An even wearier Mrs.
Portnoy followed.

Maggie told him that the Yale transcript was a fake.
She was sure of it.

The news conference on Monday was called off.
There wasn't even time to speculate as to what was to
have been announced. The polls opened at eight the
next morning.

Maggie spent most of election day calming Harley
Davis and holding Carol Gold's hand. Later she would
go to both their parties for a few minutes and then go
to the Fairmont Hotel for Portnoy's. Ironically, the
Sutter victory party was right across the street at another of the grand hotels on Nob Hill, the Mark
Hopkins. Within a stone's throw, so to speak, but of
course that would never happen. Politicians, she
thought, only threw mud.

She went home to vote in her own precinct and
didn't get there until about seven o'clock. By that
time, her vote for president was useless. The polls on
the East Coast had been closed for two hours, and the
networks had already projected sure winners. It was,
Maggie thought, one of the few handicaps about living in California. At the point where the Fifth District congressional race appeared on the ballot, she
hesitated, seriously tempted to vote for None of the
Above. What was one vote, anyway. She could only
influence one vote now. Her own. But she finally
punched the hole in the card next to Charles Portnoy,
San Francisco City Supervisor. After she had voted,

she checked with the poll judges and learned that, at this precinct, at least, there had been a good turnout. That was good for Portnoy, she knew.

She went home, changed into her green silk dress, the one that matched her eyes, and grabbed her purse. Harley's party was first, and since he couldn't lose it had started very early. The bunting was already wilting, and most of the guests were beyond standing up straight. The candidate himself was not there, according to the tradition that candidates hide themselves somewhere until the results are in. Then they could either concede or claim victory. Carol Gold's party was dreary and sad. Maggie felt sorry for her, but Carol, trouper that she was, was bucking everyone up: "Next time, next time."

Maggie reached the Fairmont about ten. The grand ballroom was filling up rapidly. It was decorated with bunting, streamers, a thousand Portnoy posters and signs. There were many bunches of red-white-and-blue balloons, and the liquor was flowing freely. A band was playing "Happy Days Are Here Again" and other songs of that ilk.

There was no doubt that this was the television age. There were large-screen TVs tuned to each network and TV Minicams following TV reporters everywhere. There was also no doubt that the Portnoy-Sutter race was the one of greatest local interest. Everyone knew already that the incumbent had been reelected president by a landslide, and the Senate race had been over before it had started.

Maggie knew a lot of people there, of course. They all treated her kindly, a little as if she'd flunked out of school. She understood why. As far as they knew, she'd been "let go." Fired. She looked around the room for Portnoy and for Fred Oliver, but neither one was there. Hiding in a room someplace, waiting to make a victory statement. Before, she would have been with them. Well, now she was just a voter, crossing her fingers for her candidate.

She fell to nursing a glass of wine, talking idly to a stranger standing beside her and half watching the television. NBC was announcing more winners on the East Coast, and now in the Midwest. It made some projections in California, stressing that the returns were not all in. The networks had been burned on projections before, by public outrage. The public did not understand how accurate polling had become, or what new methods of obtaining information had come into use, Maggie mused. NBC mentioned that in the Portnoy-Sutter race in San Francisco, no winner could be projected. It was too close.

The national news was interspersed with the local. Maggie, looking at the screen, found herself looking at a miniature picture of the room she was in, and indeed found herself in it, over the shoulder of the TV reporter. Her green dress all but glowed, she thought. Next time she was on TV she ought to wear something else. Then she wondered when next she would be on TV.

The scene switched to the ballroom of the Mark Hopkins, across the street, where the Sutter victory party was underway. It was an almost identical crowd scene, with streamers, balloons, posters and a band that caused the TV reporter to put one finger in his ear and shout into the microphone. Over *his* shoulder, Maggie saw Peter. Tanned, smiling and wearing a gray three-piece suit that looked great on camera.

Fade to the local anchors, some commercials and then announcements of other local races and propositions. In San Mateo County, Harley Davis had topped the list of supervisors by thousands of votes. In San Francisco, Carol Gold's name appeared halfway down the supervisor's candidates list—twelfth with sixty-five percent of the ballots counted. Only the top six vote getters won office. But Maggie knew some losing candidates thought that finishing twelfth the first time out was terrific. Then there was Proposition D, to raise firemen's pensions....

Maggie moved restlessly to a table where some rather pathetic hors d'oeuvres were laid out. The band lit into "Hello, Dolly," causing her to retreat to her relatively quiet place by the big-screen TV. Some more strangers were there, talking about the projections.

Maggie again divided her attention between the TV and the conversation. Her guess from the votes that were coming in was that the race was going to be very, very close. It was eleven-thirty, and the count was seesawing back and forth. This could go on all night, Maggie was thinking, when blinding lights hit her in the eyes and a microphone was shoved into her face.

"Margo Bennett, TV Mobile Four, in the Fairmont Hotel Portnoy headquarters. And you are?"

It took Maggie a moment to realize that the question was directed at her and was coming from a small, dark woman holding the microphone.

She blinked into the bright lights and managed to say her name, when she finally remembered it.

"And Maggie, what do you think of this party? Will it be victory or concession at the end?"

"Victory, of course," Maggie said loyally, still squinting.

"Were you active in Portnoy's campaign?"

"Very," Maggie assured her.

"And will you be glad when it's over?"

"Yes." Maggie was not about to explain anything, not on TV.

"Any plans afterward?"

"You bet," said Maggie. "I'm going to sail around the world. By myself, if I have to."

The reporter gave her a funny look, and said, "And now back to TV Four."

The lights went out and Maggie asked, "Was that live?" in the hope that if it was taped she could keep it off the air.

"Yes," said the cameraman. "Didn't you see yourself on the monitor?"

Maggie was glad she hadn't. The green dress. The squinting. She had been ambushed. Par for the course.

The victory party dragged on and on and on. At 1:00 a.m., people were beginning to look bedraggled. Portnoy came out on stage once to cheer everyone up, as it was far from over, he said. Nintey-five percent of the votes were in, and it was still almost even. The TV people were beginning to pack up their equipment. All the other races had been decided. There was nothing to report, except that in races this close there was usually a recount.

Maggie, on her second glass of wine, grateful that the band had seemingly given up and gone home, decided to stick it out. She was leaning on a table when suddenly she looked up to see Peter's face in a close-up on the screen. She recognized the voice of the interviewer, the same one who had ambushed her. She was even asking the same questions. Desperation to fill time, Maggie thought. Behind Peter, the crowd at the Mark Hopkins looked as weary as the one around Maggie. But Peter, for some reason, looked fresh as a spring day.

He was saying, "Yes, I'll be glad it's over."

"Do you have any plans for afterward?"

"Well, I had some until I saw you interview that woman in the green dress over at the Fairmont," Peter said. "I changed my mind. If she'll meet me in the Tonga Room in five minutes, I'll sail around the world with her."

Maggie headed for the door.

Chapter Fourteen

The only word that summed up the Tonga Room was "Really!" Maggie thought as she looked around for Peter. It was once the Fairmont's swimming pool, now converted into a Polynesian jungle, with a band that floated on an island in the middle of the pool.

But Peter came up behind her. He, after all, had had to cross the street.

The place looked packed, and there was a line, but Peter slipped a bill to the maître d' and said, "Someplace dark, please."

"We've lots of those, sir," he said, respectfully leading them to a table nearly covered with encroaching jungle in the back.

That must have been a *big* bill, Maggie thought.

Peter leaned across the table, took both of Maggie's hands and said, "You were right."

At the exact same time, Maggie said, "You were right."

Then they smiled at each other for a while, and Peter said, "When do you want to leave? Round the world, I mean."

"Now," said Maggie.

A waiter who had been standing at the table, evidently for some time, said, "Ahem. Your order?"

Peter picked up the drink menu, which was standing upright in a clear plastic holder, and held it toward the candle on the table so that he could make out what was on it.

"Maggie, do you want a Fiji Fandango, a Tiki Tiki Boo Boo, a Tahiti Sweetie or a New Guinea Nightmare? I think they all come with cucumbers in them."

Maggie decided on a white wine, and Peter on Scotch. And hold the cucumbers.

"Look, I want to have a serious discussion," Peter said. "About us. That was all kinds of fun on TV, but this is real. Do you really want to do that? Spend years out there on a small boat? Do you know what it entails?"

Maggie nodded.

"Do you want to leave San Francisco and politics and everything? It might be permanent, you know. We might get to Bora Bora and want to stay."

Maggie nodded, dreamily thinking how beautiful he was, and how beautiful Bora Bora was supposed to be. "Sixteen degrees, thirty minutes south, one hundred fifty-one degrees, forty-five minutes west," she said.

"For heaven's sake, what's that?" Peter said.

"That's where Bora Bora is. Madagascar, on the other hand, is forty-six degrees—"

"Where did you learn that?" Peter was astounded.

"I just finished a class in celestial navigation, and I have my course all charted out."

"When did you take a course in celestial navigation?"

"As soon as you said you wanted a wife who could navigate and jury-rig a sail and bench-press five hundred pounds," Maggie said.

Peter sat stunned for a few moments, then looked up at Maggie. "Well, can you?"

"Can I what?"

"Bench-press five hundred pounds?"

They talked a little about the campaign, but Maggie discovered she didn't care much. Peter guessed that she might have intervened with Portnoy about the Yale transcript, and she said she had, but she had no idea if that was the reason they had canceled the press conference. Peter confessed that he had talked to Bill Sutter about those awful ads, but he didn't know if they were pulled because of him, or because of the lower polls, or anything.

They looked at each other across the table, their drinks untouched, holding hands, until the band took a break. When all was quiet in the room, the lights dimmed even more and flashes from a strobe light shot around the room. There was a rumble of fake thunder, and a fake rainstorm poured down around the pool and by the walls. The raindrops hit the oversize leaves of the polystyrene plant beside them and splattered on the table, on Maggie and on Peter.

Peter tossed another bill on the table, pulled Maggie up and looked down at her feet. "You've got your shoes on. Good, let's go."

Out on the street, it was a perfect night. They were at the very top of Nob Hill, and the grand hotels were ablaze with lights. A couple in evening clothes was getting into a limo under the elegant porte cochere of the Mark Hopkins. The city dropped away below them, and a cable car was slowly climbing upward. A block away, the Gothic towers of soaring Grace Cathedral rose to the starry sky.

"Look, there's Polaris." Maggie pointed.

"Who cares?" said Peter, wrapping her in his arms and picking her up off the sidewalk. Then he dropped his mouth on hers, and she was lost in the stars.

In the morning, Portnoy was ahead by 157 votes, with one hundred percent of the precincts counted. Sutter demanded a recount. This surprised no one, but chagrined many. Sutter petitioned for, and was granted by the court, a total manual recount, including the spoiled ballots. Russell Travis, the registrar of voters, shrugged, said, "Well, if he's got the money..." and set the process in motion. It would take two weeks, he reckoned.

It became de rigeur in certain circles to hang around the registrar's office, peering over the shoulders of the teams of vote counters. Portnoy was there occasionally, Fred Oliver more often. Even Sutter showed up once or twice. Maggie, never having seen a total recount before, went once and quickly realized that her presence was neither help nor hindrance and that she couldn't tell anything until it was done. She never went back. Ted went, complained that a manual count was certain to produce more errors than a computer count and came up with a formula for the probability of error.

Peter and Maggie, of course, went sailing at the first opportunity, and now it was Maggie who was in charge. Sailing was iffy in November, because that was the month that the first killer storms usually came in off the North Pacific. But November could also be perfect, if it set its mind to it. And it had, this day. It was positively balmy behind Angel Island, where Maggie had moored *Maria*, at the exact spot from which she had begun her walk home from the middle of the Bay six months before. It being a weekday, *Maria* was the only boat there.

Maggie was lying on her back, with her head on a life jacket. "Did you really consider giving up sailing around the world?" she asked. "I'm not sure I believe you."

Peter was lying next to her on his stomach, with his head on his crossed arms. "Yes, I really did."

"But why? I don't understand."

"You didn't seem to want to go."

"You never asked me."

"I didn't need to. You had me convinced that the right thing to do was stay here and get involved in elections. The nuclear sub, remember?"

"Wasn't there some other reason?" Maggie asked disingenuously. She knew there was, and what it was, but she just wanted to hear him say it again.

"Yeah," he said. "I couldn't leave Genghis Khat."

Maggie stuck her tongue out at him. "You almost had me convinced that anything legal goes in an election."

"And you changed my mind. Some," Peter said. "But look how it turned out, after all that money was spent and all that pain, agony and argument: they're fighting over a hundred and fifty votes."

"But it will come out all right in the end. Somebody will win. Unlike Rincon. Everybody lost there."

"Not necessarily. Rincon was going down the tubes no matter what. Think of the stockholders and the employees. Maybe what happened is the best thing. Certainly, I'm glad it's over."

"At least," she said, "this election is one where one vote really means something."

"Do you really think," Peter said, "that things would have been any different if Sutter hadn't run those dirty ads, or if Portnoy had released that fake transcript?"

"I don't know. Nobody ever really knows. Who knows what any one man thinks in the privacy of the voting booth?"

"I hope I know," Peter said. "I hope he thinks of his principles. I hope he thinks of his conscience. I hope he makes moral judgments. Just like one campaign consultant I know did."

"Are you saying you don't believe that all is fair in love and war anymore?"

Peter thought about that for a long time.

Then he said, "I'll amend that. It only applies to love."

He reached for her and she reached for him, and they met in the middle and kissed. The boat rocked, the tip of the mast swinging in a fifteen-degree arc, for a long time.

On the next run across the Bay, they talked about sailing around the world. There were some things that needed to be done to the boat over the winter, and Peter had long before figured out what provisions were needed and where to get them. They disagreed on the course, naturally, after the Marquesas. Maggie wished to go straight to Tahiti and Bora Bora, and Peter wanted to island-hop. But they both wanted to see Tonga, so they agreed to disagree, at least until they reached Marquesas.

"What are you going to do about Ted?" Peter asked. "After all, you're closing down and giving up your office."

"Oh, Ted," Maggie said. "Not to worry. He's going to work for Mervin Field, the pollster. He's thrilled. *They* called him. What are you going to do about Genghis Khat?"

"I don't know yet. I'm sure I can find somebody to take him." Peter looked thoughtful. "He's kind of a problem placement."

"Ted will take him," Maggie promised. She thought a minute. "Peter, who is Maria?"

He looked slightly annoyed. "I've tried to tell you—I don't know. It was the name on the boat when I got her."

Maggie laughed. "There was a time when I was convinced that Maria was your lost love, or your wife or something. I was jealous."

"I never knew that," he said. "Haven't you noticed something different lately about the boat?"

"No," said Maggie.

"Hang out over the transom and look at the name."

Maggie leaned out as far as she dared over the back end of the boat and looked. "When did you do that?"

"A long time ago. I guess I knew it all along."

The name Maria was gone. What Maggie saw, by hanging upside down over the end of the boat, was:

San Francisco
MAGGIE, TOO

The wedding was in the small but magnificent side chapel at Grace Cathedral. The sun streamed in the tall, narrow stained-glass windows, spangling the thirteenth-century carved stone altar. A cable-car bell had nearly drowned out the light Bach cantata played by the organist.

The Honorable Charles Portnoy, Congressman-elect for the Fifth District of the State of California—by 203 votes—gave the bride away. The best man was William Sutter, who was also throwing the reception at the St. Francis Yacht Club, to which his family had belonged for a hundred years. He was nervously eyeing the old-line city-hall pols who filled the hand-

carved wooden pews behind the bride and groom,
thinking of the bar bill.

The bride, though radiant, was nervous, too,
through the first words of the ceremony, anyway.

"Dearly beloved," began the priest. Maggie held
her breath.

". . . into this holy union Margaret and Peter now
come to be joined." Here it is, thought Maggie.

"If any of you can show just cause why they may
not lawfully be married, speak now, or else forever
hold your peace."

There was a long pause.

Ted didn't say a thing—for the first time in his life,
Maggie figured. There would be no retribution today,
at any rate, for her making him take Genghis Khat, the
twenty-pound difficult adoption.

"Margaret, will you have this man . . ." the priest
finally continued.

Maggie let her breath out. She glanced over at Peter on her left. He looked gorgeous in his morning
coat. He was gazing very seriously at the priest. She
decided to keep him, and said so, right out loud in
church.

*   *   *   *   *

ATTRACTIVE, SPACE SAVING BOOK RACK

Display your most prized novels on this handsome and sturdy book rack. The hand-rubbed walnut finish will blend into your library decor with quiet elegance, providing a practical organizer for your favorite hard-or soft-covered books.

Only $9.95

Approximately 16" x 8" when assembled

Assembles in seconds!

To order, rush your name, address and zip code, along with a check or money order for $10.70* ($9.95 plus 75¢ postage and handling) payable to *Silhouette Books*.

Silhouette Books
Book Rack Offer
901 Fuhrmann Blvd.
P.O. Box 1396
Buffalo, NY 14269-1396

Offer not available in Canada.

*New York and Iowa residents add appropriate sales tax.

BKR-2A

Silhouette Romance

COMING NEXT MONTH

#616 TO MARRY AT CHRISTMAS—Kasey Michaels
Elizabeth Chatham wasn't looking for romance... until she met
dynamic Nicholas Lancaster and fell head over heels. Would
wedding bells harmonize with sleigh bells?

#617 AFTER THE STORM—Joan Smith
Aspiring writer Susan Knight was more than curious about her
mysterious new neighbor, Dan Ogilvy. She had to discover what
the sexiest man she'd ever met was up to....

#618 IF DREAMS WERE WILD HORSES—Adeline McElfresh
Ana-Maureen Salem thought she was fenced into her city life. But
then she bought a wild horse and met Jeremy Rodriguez—the one
man who could let her passion run free!

#619 THE KERANDRAON LEGACY—Sara Grant
The legacy of a magnificent Breton mansion stood between them,
but one magical moonlit night Christie Beaumont lost her heart
forever to devastating Luc Keraven....

#620 A MAN OF HER OWN—Brenda Trent
Widow Kaye Wilson dreamed of building a life for herself and
her daughter—without the help of a man. Then she met
irresistible Whit Brooks....

#621 CACTUS ROSE—Stella Bagwell
Years after he'd left her, rugged Tony Ramirez returned to help
lovely Andrea Rawlins save her ranch. Could Andrea risk loving
this masterful Texan again?

AVAILABLE THIS MONTH:

FOUR UNIQUE SERIES FOR EVERY WOMAN YOU ARE..

Silhouette Romance

Love, at its most tender, provocative, emotional... in stories that will make you laugh and cry while bringing you the magic of falling in love.

6 titles per month

Silhouette Special Edition

Sophisticated, substantial and packed with emotion, these powerful novels of life and love will capture your imagination and steal your heart.

6 titles per month

Silhouette Desire

Open the door to romance and passion. Humorous, emotional, compelling—yet always a believable and sensuous story—Silhouette Desire never fails to deliver on the promise of love.

6 titles per month

Silhouette Intimate Moments

Enter a world of excitement, of romance heightened by suspense, adventure and the passions every woman dreams of. Let us sweep you away.

4 titles per month